Moonlight Rogues: Origins

A Moonlight Rogues Novella

By Alexa Whitewolf

Moonlight Rogues: Origins
A Moonlight Rogues Novella
by Alexa Whitewolf

Copyright ©2019 Alexa Whitewolf

Cover design by **Y. Nikolova at Ammonia Book Covers**

First Edition

This is a work of fiction.

Names, characters, places, and incidents either are the product of the author's imagination or are used fictitiously, and any resemblance to actual persons, living or dead, business establishments, events, or locales is entirely coincidental.

Author's Note & Acknowledgements

Most of my books start from dreams. It so happened with *First to Fall* (Moonlight Rogues, #1), that after years of avoiding the paranormal romance genre, I was sucked in by a very demanding wolf – Dominic Kosta. And as his story developed, so did Tristan's, Finn's, and Lucas'. And I ended up with another series!

Make no mistake: these wolves are not easy to understand. They're complex, standoffish at times, but good at their core. Each deals with a past that's not all cut and dry, and it doesn't help that that they each come from various cultural background – with their own demons, superstitions, and enemies. To top it off? These wolves are fiercely protective of their mates, which more often than not lands them into trouble.

So when Dom's story was done, I thought that was it. He'd show up in the subsequent books, add to the plot, and then they'd all they get their happily ever after. Well, my wolves had other ideas. Nights of constant repeat dreams of their "before" stories resulted in, well, me giving in.

Hence, I present you *Moonlight Rogues: Origins*. A compilation of four short stories depicting the wolves' journeys before they all knew each other... And *way* before their adventures in Rockland Creek. Plus, you'll also see aspects of various types of werewolves. Each one of my wolves has a particular power/ability and folkloric background. Though I'm only giving you enough here to whet the appetite, you'll learn more about their in-depth strengths throughout the series. And for any of my Romanian fans, you may find a fun surprise at the end... Ileana Cosânzeana and Făt Frumos are characters in Romanian folklore similar to a good witch and Prince Charming, and they do make an appearance in my series ☺

Also, at the end of each short story, you'll get a chance to either skip to the preview for their actual book, or you'll find a link to my website, where each book has its purchase links. Signing up for my newsletter will also get you a discount to apply towards purchase ☺

One last note before I move on to the acknowledgements: these short stories, and the books that follow them, are for an 18+ audience. While the short stories are devoid of sex, they do contain swearing and violence. The books depict sex scenes (not erotica), and contain swearing as well. Some deal with rougher subjects like PTSD and mental health, as well. It is never my intention to offend anyone, hence why I'm providing this little heads up.

Now, to the best part! I want to give a HUGE thanks to my mom for encouraging me; to my husband for his never-ending support and curiosity about this series; to my furbabies, for being a constant source of inspiration; to the editing and beta reading them – thank you!!! Special kudos to Y. Nikolova with Ammonia Book Covers, for the epic cover!

And last but not least, thanks to my readers!

Happy readings,

Alexa

∞ ∞ ∞

A BLOOD PRICE

~Lucas

"Luciano, andiamo!"

His father's irate voice jolted him out of bed in the middle of the night. Luciano blinked at the ceiling, a low rumble building in his chest. In the darkness, his eyes flashed with coal fire, before he became fully awake and reined his wolf in.

He had seconds, if only, to rub the sleep out of his eyes and pull on a shirt and sweatpants. The pack's alpha – and the family's head – did not recognize excuses, and lateness counted as an error in judgement.

The door swung open, and Luciano's youngest brother poked his head through. "Ma cosa stanno facendo?" Matteo whispered sleepily, demanding to know what all the fuss was about.

Luciano shrugged and stepped to him, wrapping his arm around his shoulders. "Go back to sleep, Matt," he whispered in English. "It's me they want."

Once assured Matteo was back in bed, Luciano headed downstairs. He had to descend two flights of stairs, surrounded by opulence and luxury at each corner. Even the clothes he wore were brand name. Their mansion was huge – his father liked such things. It allowed him to host massive parties, hiding the dealings taking place under the authorities' very noses.

Not that it mattered. With his group of Mafiosi, Alessandro Conti had the entire city under his control, either through fear, or bribery. Or both.

When he reached downstairs, Luciano looked around, frowning. "Where the hell are they?"

Gunshots outside drew his attention, but did not jolt him. The sound was familiar, an old friend, one could say. He'd been twelve the first time his father had shown him how to handle a gun. At thirteen, he'd held a man at gunpoint to save Alessandro. To this day, he didn't know if it had been a good choice, or whether he should have let the bastard – his father – deal with his fate alone.

And yet, Luciano hadn't. And life had gone on – except for the culprit, who'd been apprehended and dealt with accordingly. Alessandro Conti did not take kindly to rebellion.

Shaking his head, Luciano walked through the ballroom, then the sunroom, passed by the kitchen to nick an apple, and ended by the massive patio. French doors surrounded a breathtaking view where sunrise and lake met for a little piece of paradise.

Paradise, or hell?

Inside him, an urge nagged at him. Luciano's wolf wanted to roam free. Since he'd dropped his university degree in entrepreneurship and returned home, Alessandro had been demanding. Meetings every day, sometimes more than once. All to better initiate him, to get him ready to take the reins of a Mafia empire he wanted nothing to do with.

And among those, his wolf was cornered, limited, having to…*obey.*

At only twenty-five, Luciano was nowhere ready for the responsibility that came with leading Alessandro's empire. And despite what had happened ten years earlier, he loathed guns with a passion. His wolf, on the other hand, relished the violence – the control. And the more it got restrained, the more he wanted to rip through his skin, to own the man, to prove himself.

Lately, it took all of Luciano's mental energy to hold him back. And with each passing day, the motivation to do so ebbed further and further away.

He wanted nothing more than to run, to leave it all behind. If it hadn't been for his mother and younger brother, he would have. They alone kept him tied to the place, and to the master of the domain – his father.

Thoughts of escaping came to a stop as his eyes stopped taking in the scenery, and instead noticed his mother, Francesca. Like a lonely ghost, she stood at the patio entrance, dressed in nothing but her dark satin nightgown and robe. She stared at something in the distance and, judging by her tense back, whatever it was bothered her.

"What's going on?"

She turned to him with a heavy sigh. Long, flaming locks framed a heart-shaped face, full lips, and eyes of honey. Francesca was a queen in her own right, yet her beauty had aged with time.

"The usual." The glint in her eyes faded some more when she noticed he was dressed and on his way out. "*Non piu.* Do not be like him, Luciano. I raised you better than this."

Luciano took a step closer, cupping her cheek. He towered over her by a head, and each passing day Francesca seemed frailer. Searching her eyes, he looked for the deeper meaning to her words – only a flash of red answered him, a reminder she held her own haunting power.

In the end, he nodded and kissed his mother's forehead, then headed onto the grounds. Noises in the distance perked his ears – his father was talking to two men, who held a third on his knees.

It was time for blood.

∞ ♦ ∞

"So, what did Papà want this morning?"

Luciano ignored his brother's questioning gaze, and instead tossed the football back at him. "Your turn."

Matteo wasn't so keen to let go. He caught the ball, feinted to the left, then right, and ran past his brother, only to be body-checked midway. With a grunt, he fell to the grass, the ball bouncing out of his hand.

Luciano towered over him, grinning. "Watch yourself, fratello. You know we play in this familia to win."

Matteo rolled his eyes. "As if I didn't know that already." He ignored Luciano's offered hand and stood, picking up the ball. His stance informed his brother he was done playing around. "What did he want?"

Luciano's jaw clenched. "You want no part in this, Matteo. Believe me."

His younger brother raised his chin defiantly. "And if I do? I'm eighteen now, more than old enough. I'm older than *you* were when papà dragged you in this."

Luciano looked away. "It wasn't by my choice."

"But I want to."

"No, *idiota*, you fucking don't!" Matteo's innocent determination was too much, snapping his restraint. Luciano grabbed him by the scruff of his shirt, pulling him close. Baring his teeth, nostrils flaring, he shouted in his face, "Do you not understand the price of all this blood?"

Seeing his brother's blanching face, Luciano let him go. "What do you think I do all day, hmm? Play house? This morning, dear Papà had me deliver punishment to a man I don't even know was truly guilty. He plays God, jury and executioner in one. And we, my foolish fratello, we are his executioners. It is on our souls the mark stays."

Matteo stared at him a beat. Thoughts swirled in his honey-colored eyes, so like their mother's, until it finally clicked. "Is that what you're afraid of? The promise of hell that priest goes on and on about?"

Luciano laughed – a cold, bitter sound. "I care nothing for the priest, fratello. But what he speaks of, it's not all fiction. I've seen it. And I've no intention of ever ending there."

Before Matteo could press further, Luciano walked away, the game long forgotten. His steps turned into lunges, then he was flat-out running. Before long, his wolf was too pressing, too demanding, and he let him out.

The urge was dark, chaotic – an escape from what he perceived as freedom. Clothes ripped from his body, agony burned through him, but still he didn't stop until a russet-colored wolf had taken the man's shape, dashing across the grounds.

It was nighttime by the time Luciano returned home. Servants had long left the grounds – they had strict orders not to stick around after sunset. Alessandro wanted them to know as little as possible about the family's true lineage, but rumors still persisted. Luciano had heard them in the surrounding villages, and learned to ignore them.

So what if he came from a family of lupi mannari? So what if all stories of their kind ended in bloodshed, and innocent lives lost? He hadn't chosen to be born a werewolf – but it was the hand fate had dealt him. And he didn't intend to turn his back on it.

A shadow moved, and he froze on his way across the marble floors. "Mother?"

Francesca stepped out of the shadows. Her eyes had a feverish glaze to them, and her skin was flushed, yet she spoke clearly. "Did you let your wolf run free tonight?"

"I did."

She nodded, and said nothing else for a long moment. Then, a weary sigh escaped her, and her petite frame trembled in its entirety. "What did you and Matteo fight about this afternoon?"

Luciano shook his head. "He's being a fool, Mamma. Wants to join the business, thinks he's ready at eighteen."

A flash of panic crossed Francesca's face. "No! You cannot let him." She was on him in a flash, her nails digging into the flesh of his biceps. "Luciano, non piu! I cannot have another son condemned so."

"Then *tell him*!" Luciano whispered. "Tell him what you are, so he'll finally understand why he cannot! I tried to explain the cost today, but he thinks they're ramblings of a religious fool."

Tears escaped Francesca's eyes, but still she shook her head. "He cannot, Luciano."

"And I can only do so much to stop him, Mamma. If I keep fighting him on this, Matteo might believe I don't want the competition. Ironic, isn't it? When the truth is if it wasn't for him and you, I would have left a long, long time ago." He gritted his teeth, and whispered harshly, "I can live with my sins and whatever the afterlife has in store for *me*, alone."

A pale hand rose to his cheek, and he nuzzled into it. "Mamma, please. Tell him."

Francesca stepped away, nodding. "I will. Tomorrow." A look behind him at the full moon, and she sighed once more. "Rest well, mio figlio."

Morning came by too soon. Luciano woke up from another dream of fire and hell. He wished, not for the first time, that his mother had not revealed her connection to the Underworld. Especially since his fate was already sealed, thanks to his father's business.

Refusing to spend time on things he could not change, he dragged himself out of bed and went by his morning run. An hour later, he wandered back in the still-empty house.

As he showered, Luciano wondered about his father's absence. It was not usual for Alessandro to take a day "off" his job. Rather, it never happened.

Sensing something else was amiss, he headed back downstairs. Alessandro was already seated in the dining area, at the head of their massive mahogany table. A servant dropped a plate of breakfast in front of him, before turning her attention to Luciano. "And for you, signore?"

"The same will do, grazie."

Ignoring the ravenous grumblings of his stomach, Luciano sipped some black coffee. "Where is mother?"

Alessandra turned another page of the newspaper, and pushed his empty cup aside. He spoke without looking up. "Prego, Luciano. Your nonchalant tone does not fool me. She is unwell, and will not be joining us today."

Luciano's wolf poked its head at the lie. If nothing else in the trade, he'd learned how to smell a liar a mile away. And though his father was masterful at it, he could no longer hide it from him.

Matteo's entrance stopped further interrogation from taking place. He took a seat opposite Luciano, on their father's other side, and the servant hurried with his breakfast.

His honey gaze roamed over Alessandro, then finally turned to Luciano. A faint smile graced his lips. "Sorry about yesterday, Lucas."

Luciano nodded at the nickname, returning the smile. "Bygones, fratello. Have you spoken to mother?"

"No, why?"

A rustle of newspaper, and Alessandro glanced at his sons. "As I've already mentioned to Luciano, Francesca is indisposed. She will be bedridden for most of the day."

He went back to his newspaper once more. The doorbell ringing drew everyone's gazes upwards. Alessandro nodded at the butler waiting by the entrance. "Go let him in." To his sons, he said, "And you two, behave."

Like dogs, Luciano thought darkly.

His wolf rumbled some more, trying to test the limits of his endurance. With an ever-darkening gaze, Luciano watched his father's not-sodisinterested expression. *It would be so easy, to take it all... He wouldn't even see me coming. I have the one gift he cannot control.*

As if catching his thoughts, Alessandro looked up from the newspaper. His onyx eyes met mirrored images in Luciano's, and they stared at each other for a beat. Then Matteo cleared his throat, and Luciano looked away.

Pushing his pride – and much too eager wolf – aside, he focused on the entrance, interested to see who was joining them. His father rarely had day business meetings in the house. Not long ago, the local police had taken a keen interest and set up surveillance – before Alessandro had bought them off. He'd been careful ever since, and kept illicit dealings for his balls and parties.

The butler returned, and behind him was a man of Alessandro's height, though broader in shoulders. He wore a suit that smelled of money, and his cutthroat gaze went straight for the head of the house.

"Alessandro, ciao!" As the men shook hands, Luciano and Matteo watched with curiosity.

"Ricci, glad you could make it. These are my sons, Luciano and Matteo."

The newcomer spared them a glance, then his gaze landed on Alessandro once more and his tone changed. "Why the summons?"

"I've received word of a deal happening tonight, and I intend to take over it. Those South-

American pricks will not be running drugs on mio territorio. Not while I can help it."

Ricci rubbed his jaw, glanced at the brothers once more. "And why do you need me?"

"I'll run two operations. Luciano will come with me, and I want you to take Matteo. It's about time he's introduced to the familia – properly."

The dread growing in Luciano's stomach exploded and he kicked the chair out from under him. Slamming his palms on the table, he growled, "No!"

Matteo's shocked gaze met his over the table. "I-I can do it."

"You shouldn't have to," Luciano spit, clenching his fists some more. The change was rumbling over his body, the wolf wanting to let loose. Whatever restraint he'd had, was long gone. This was about to become a contest – one for power, for control. And his wolf had no intention of losing it.

Alessandro's nostrils flared. "You would go against your papà?"

"Yes," Luciano gritted out. "Matteo is too untrained for this."

"He will learn."

Luciano took a step closer, barely controlling his grip on the change. "Not like this."

Alessandro turned to face him fully. For a big man, he moved with the speed of a cheetah. The slap came so hard, it knocked Luciano into the wall. A paint clattered to the ground, at the same time as the son.

"*Basta!* Learn your place, idiota."

Dismissing him as easily as an insect, Alessandro turned to Ricci. On one knee, Luciano glared at their backs. Fists clenched, he tried to pull in deep breaths. *This is not the way to do it. Not tonight.*

Matteo stood to come to his aid, but Alessandro gave him a withering look. "Sit still."

Matteo hesitated, glancing at his brother. Luciano shook his head a fraction, signaling for him to listen to the command. Then he scrambled up to his feet, and wiped the blood from the corner of his mouth. *The old bastardo still has strength left in him. At least when it comes to hurting his sons.*

He turned to walk away, trembling with held back rage. Each step was a fight – against his pride, against his wolf, against everything he'd been taught.

And just as he reached the door, Alessandro's voice came from behind. "I expect you to be there tonight."

Luciano didn't answer, instead clenching his fists and forcing his body through the exit before he did something he would regret.

∞ ♦ ∞

Luciano spent the afternoon trying to figure out a solution, a way to protect Matteo when their father had already set a path for him – just as he'd done for his first born.

Unable to hold still any longer, he went out for another run. Not even his wolf could calm him down, and he burned with the need to take over his father's alpha role. Some of his men were human, some wolf, but they would all answer to him. Luciano knew it, deep down.

Was he ready to take the step? Was he ready to get so neck-deep into the whole business? Or would it be better to let it die on its own?

He got back home in time to see black cars leaving the premises, their heavy tires creaking over gravel. Inside the house, Francesca waited at the top of the stairs, wringing her hands. "Why did Matteo go with them?"

Blinding rage consumed him, and he stomped up halfway. "Where were you all day? You were supposed to have talked to him!"

Francesca shook her head, holding onto the railing. "I had a migraine in the morning, and by the time I woke up, your father locked me in the room. He gave strict orders to the servants."

Luciano stepped up some more. "And you couldn't have escaped? Called out for help?"

The glare she leveled on him stopped him in his tracks. "You know that is not how things are done in this pack."

A growl escaped him through bared teeth. "Then perhaps it's time for a new leader."

Francesca's lips parted in disbelief. "You would do that? Take over? You know there is but one way…"

"Yes. Father would have to die, by my hand. There are no half measures with him."

Her gaze was not as horrified as he feared. Rather, she seemed to assess the confidence behind his words. "And you'd be ready for that?"

Luciano gritted his teeth. "Do I have a choice, Mamma? Matteo is out there being indoctrinated, maybe against his will. His soul will pay the same price mine already does." He shook his head. "This could have been avoided if you'd told us the truth earlier."

"You really think so?" Francesca scoffed. "When your father found out I have Chimera blood in me, he was outraged. A wife with not only a connection to the Underworld, but with the power to open the gates of Hell itself? It wasn't until he witnessed the power in me that he stopped seeing me as an omen for disaster, and instead as an asset. He cared not for the toll his killings have on his soul – or mine. How could I have known you two would not follow in his footsteps?"

Luciano took another step closer. "It was my right to know I have a direct link to the Underworld. It was *my* right to decide whether taking lives was a stain I wanted on my soul, when each innocent death brought me that much closer to becoming the monster of legend. It was my *choice*, and you took it from me when you kept your silence!"

Months of frustration built in him, and he clenched his fists. Luciano would never raise a hand against his mother – or any woman – but the rage unfurling in him was pushing his boundaries.

Francesca stepped closer to him, tears shining in her eyes. "I am sorry, mio figlio. I never meant to cause you harm, or pain. Please believe me. I had hoped to avoid this curse, thinking perhaps you only had your father's werewolf genes in you, but…"

Luciano's coal eyes met hers. "But I don't. You can tell me the truth, he's not here to hear it. I took after him, yes, but more so after you. And the Chimera blood in me could overpower him. *Will* overpower him, if I choose to use it." He inhaled sharply then, and bitterness seeped his last words. "Unless I lose myself to the monster, and become forever a pawn of the Underworld."

The truth shone in his mother's eyes, and he did not need any further confirmation. Her trembling hand lifted to his chest.

"Go with them, ti scongiuro," Francesca whispered. "I beg you. You can protect Matteo."

Luciano glanced up from the ground. "Only for father to do it all over again?"

Her eyes flashed, and for the first time he saw someone else. "Mamma?"

Francesca's voice was deeper when she spoke, her eyes filled with a fire not all her own. "Your inaction will spill blood tonight, my son. *Go.* Before it is too late."

∞ ♦ ∞

The Maserati drove like the wind – swift, slick, racing between the streets. Luciano speed-dialed his brother once more, but the call went to voicemail. Again.

He knew the location of the drop, but he'd wanted to try and convince his brother to get out of there while he still could. Giving up on the idea, he gunned the engine.

After breaking every traffic law imaginable, Luciano pulled up in the port. An industrial ship had already thrown anchor, and two groups of men were facing each other – one aboard, the other on the ground.

Among them, he found his brother's red locks, beside Ricci. Alessandro's closest men, his A team, he could see on the boat, trying to overtake the other group from behind. It was a smart strategy, except for one obvious drawback: it placed his brother smack in the middle of danger. On the front lines, so to speak. Part of him wondered for a split second if their father had done it on purpose. The other part discounted the notion, and charged through.

The Maserati slammed into a group of men trying to take aim at his father's army. Spinning without grip, Luciano gunned pulled on the stick shift and forced the car in a circle. Dust rose everywhere, confusing everyone enough to give him the distraction he'd needed.

One-handed, he threw the door open and let the car out of his control. Rolling on the ground, Luciano got up to a crouch and pulled the gun out of the waistband of his jeans.

Snip. Snip. Snip.

Left. Right. Duck. Behind. He knew where his enemies were with uncanny accuracy. Deadly like the darkest of ghouls, he made his way through the lines, trying to cut a clear path to his brother.

Then a shot ran in the air. The group aboard the ship opened fire back, and Matteo ducked somewhere, pulling a gun from the waistband of his shirt.

"Matteo, no!"

His brother glanced up, trying to see where the voice had come from. Luciano aimed and shot at the men more likely to harm him – then the click of an empty chamber sounded. Growling, he tossed the gun to the ground and morphed.

Humans turned at the sounds of his howls of agony, but he didn't care. Then he was stepping on paws, panting, inhaling deeply. His wolf relished the blood, the violence – sought it. And for once, Luciano didn't hold him back. He needed the wolf – the primal, the monster. Because he was the only one who could undo the whole mess.

If there was one thing Luciano was sure of, it was that his time was counted. The whole thing had been a trap, or some kind of power play, and his brother was about to pay with his life.

Even as the bullets came at him, the ground underneath him turned blurry. He was fast. Faster than he'd ever been.

Bullets ricocheted off him, straight into his enemies.

His teeth crunched into arms in his path, tore through legs that tried to stop him.

His claws elongated, scraping the ground and tearing at necks.

And still, he wasn't fast enough. Bullets rang out – once, twice.

Matteo got hit in the chest – once, twice.

He fell to his knees, and another bullet went through him, hitting the side of his neck. Luciano saw the blood spurt, and the last shred of his sanity snapped.

His inhumane snarl had most men turn to him, with mirroring expressions of confusion. He didn't care. Luciano – the wolf – attacked, tearing through the last of them, and not knowing he was playing right into his father's hands.

Not realizing it was already too late.

The distraction – his appearance – gave Alessandro's other team enough time to attack from behind, efficiently killing off all attackers. By the time Luciano got to Matteo, the damage had been done.

He morphed back to human, breaking their pack law. Yet showing the humans under his father's command his true colors was nothing compared to the pain spreading in his chest. Naked, Luciano crawled over the pavement, scraping his knees and palms, and dragged his younger brother to his chest. "Matteo...."

With glazed eyes, his brother looked at him. "You were right. This wasn't...for me. Tell Mamma... I'm sorry."

Luciano buried his face in the red locks, hot tears escaping him. Something happened then, something he could not explain. Amid the chaos of the battle, the shouts of orders rang, the confused whispers of the human men on his father's team who could not believe what they had witnessed... Among all that, Matteo's body vibrated for a few short seconds.

Though his eyes were closed, Luciano felt something on his cheek, almost a caress. Then a voice, his brother's voice, whispered, "Leave... Save yourself while you can. It's not too late for your soul."

Warmth filled him, like the cocoon of a hug, then it was gone. And another voice – a hated one – took its place.

"Get up."

Alessandro was there. Luciano glanced up into unfeeling eyes and a cold expression. A blanket was thrown over him, and men lifted him to his feet. "Matteo..."

"Leave him. They will collect him on the way home."

Weak in the knees, Luciano let them drag him. In the car on the way over, his father's look was speculative. "You have her skills, mio figlio. A delightful surprise indeed."

Passing of the dead…. The door to the Underworld… Matteo, my dear brother… Tears threatened anew, but he willed himself to show no weakness. His father would never understand what had happened. He only cared for what the Chimera's power could give him – an easy way to clear the bodies, to hide his crimes. The price it would have for Luciano – or Francesca – was not something on Alessandro's radar.

Luciano turned a glare his way. "You dare speak like that, when Matteo's body is not even cold?"

Alessandro shrugged. "That's why I had two sons, so at least one could live." They pulled in front of the house, and not soon enough. Luciano rushed out, feeling bile curl up in his throat. He threw up on the side of the house, then wiped his mouth and walked inside.

Francesca was waiting in the hallway, a hand to her throat. When she saw his face, she fell to her knees, as if her legs could no longer hold her up. Luciano would never forget that cry, that blood-curling scream, as long as he lived.

Nor would he forget waking up in the middle of the night to the sounds of arguing, followed by two gun shots.

By the time he'd gone to their bedroom, it was too late. Francesca lay in a heap on the floor, her lifeless eyes staring at him. Luciano staggered and held himself against the wall. Out of reflex, he looked around for his father – only to find him on his knees, by the bed. A bloody hand was pressed to his gut wound, and he was staring in shock at his dead wife.

"What did you *do*?" Luciano snarled. "Was one death not enough for you?"

Alessandro looked up at him then, tears streaming down his cheeks. "She... took my gun. Turned it on herself. I... Her powers, it's all gone." To himself, he whispered, "She was the last. The last one."

Luciano shook his head. Gritting his teeth against the tear in his heart, he picked up his mom off the ground and walked out of the house. Each step felt like lead, but he powered through. What was the point of crying, when no tears would bring either of them back?

On the property, lost amid all others, was a tree Francesca had treasured above all others. It was there he dug a grave with his own hands, then laid her inside, wrapped in the satin bed sheets she liked.

Wiping at his face, Luciano then walked inside the house.

∞ ♦ ∞

That morning, before the sun was even up, Luciano packed a bag, some money and took off. Dropped his car in the middle of nowhere, hopped on a bus, and didn't look back. There would be no way to trace him, no way to know where he'd gone. He had to leave, because what he wanted to do to his father…

For Matteo, for Francesca, he wouldn't. Not now. Maybe not ever.

At least, I can make sure he doesn't use me, too.

Luciano didn't even check the destination on his ticket. All he wanted was to get as far away as possible. With each bus station, he bought another ticket. And another. Two days later, a half-empty bus pulled up in the middle of nowhere.

By the time he got to Rockland Creek, he was done with his old life, with his name, with his legacy. He was done with love, with women, with caring. From now on, it would be each man for himself, and nothing more.

On foot, he walked to the closest diner and ordered food. His wolf thanked him – he'd starved him too much – and he made a deal with himself then and there. No one would ever contest him, no one would take control from him ever again.

When the waitress asked him for his name, he answered without blinking – an alias. "Lucas Bianchi."

The past was meant to be buried. And love…was an inconvenience. As for the powers inherited from his mother, one thing rang true: his soul was already doomed. Redemption was not for him, not in this life – or the next.

And as he ate his food, and drank his whiskey, the lupo mannaro shed the last of his skin. The boy he'd been disappeared, replaced by the man he would then become. Luciano Conti was gone, buried in the past.

If only the past would stay buried, too…

Turn to page 153 for a preview

of Lucas' story!

∞ ∞ ∞

A NEW BEGINNING

~Dominic

Mountains the size of the sky.

Air so pure it scorched the lungs.

Water so clear it called for a swim.

And above all…the smell of meat.

Dominic knew nothing but the thrill of the run. He didn't realize it when his body changed – nor what truly had happened.

All he knew was the chase – grass under his feet.

The crave – mouth-watering scents in the air.

And then…the crunch under his teeth.

Metallic taste hit his tongue, and snapped him out of the trance. Then he was back on two feet, shaking, and wondering at his naked state. The dead deer under him looked up through lifeless eyes. His bloodied hands hinted at what had happened.

Dominic cried then...for a long time. It was not the first time he'd felt the urge in his chest, but it was the first it had completely taken over. Though he was only five years old, he knew enough not to let the meat go to waste. So he wiped off his tears, and pulled the carcass over his shoulders. Blood from its wounds – where his canine teeth had bitten – trickled down his back. Yet the deer's body was light – lighter than a feather. Guilt for having taken its life choked him.

Step by step, he walked back home. He didn't really know the two people who'd taken him in, as they had every orphan in the region. Whispers abounded the children were no good, that they were cursed, but still, the two adults were nice. Firm, but they provided food on the table and a shelter.

After what he'd been through, it was more than he expected. After all, how could he want more, when he'd lost everything so young?

A few more steps. The thickness of the forest gave way to a valley, and smoke rose from a chimney he knew only too well. Dominic walked down, paying little attention to the scratches on his feet. With each step, he forgot about the crime, lost some of the guilt – until he saw their faces.

The guardians were waiting by the door. And when they saw his bloodied face, the deer on his shoulders, and his complete nakedness, the woman fell to her knees and prayed. The man crossed himself, then gulped and held a crucifix in his hand, clenched so tightly his knuckles whitened. Keeping his distance, he directed Dominic to the shed where he could put the deer.

For the first time that night, Dominic was not allowed around the other children. Instead, he slept under the stars. It wouldn't be the last, and he wouldn't know a safe home again until an American couple adopted him a year later.

18 years later…

"Dominic, why?"

His adoptive mother stared at him with tears in her eyes. Her husband – his father – remained silent, resigned to the outcome.

Dominic sighed, ran a hand through his hair and tried to figure out a way to communicate his emotions. The couple facing him had adopted him since he'd been young, caught in the wild and brought to an orphanage after his last parents had given him up. He owed them everything.

His cushy life. The trust fund. The vet school.

And now, at only twenty-four, he was throwing it all away... without much explanation. They deserved better, he knew it.

Their confusion and hurt was evident, and he cared for them. He did. Just…not enough to stay and be molded into the kind of citizen they wanted. The only thing he could say to ease their worries was what wouldn't hurt them. That he'd visit. That he'd stay in touch.

That… "I don't belong here."

And that, in a nutshell, was the truth.

Despite the tutors. Despite the years. Despite all the time and effort, he was no more a part of their world than they were of his.

Dominic had learned to dress like them, learned to talk like them. His accent was gone, buried under years of molding his voice to ensure he wasn't too different. So much had changed, yet nothing had erased the hunger in him. The need to survive. The need to be the best. The belief there was something – some*one* – out there for him. Something made just for him.

Not gifted. Not given. Made *for him*.

Dominic looked into their eyes, his blonde locks falling in his blue eyes, and he smiled. "I love you both. And I know you don't understand. But I need this... I need to go."

He was right, they didn't understand. But they loved him, so they nodded and gave their blessing. The next day, he left with a backpack, a stack of cash, and nothing more.

∞ ♦ ∞

On a farm, middle of nowhere...

"Stai! Stop! Don't pull!" Dominic's shout was harsh, Romanian orders escaping him out of reflex, until he switched back to English. The cow's poor howling had jolted him out sleep and he'd run over, thinking it was in danger.

The poor farmer who's taken him in for the night looked up from the cow's legs, sweat beading his face and blood all over his hands. "She needs to birth!"

Dominic lifted his hands, palms facing outward, and slowly inched closer. "Let me help."

The man frowned. Dominic knew what must be going through his mind. How could a homeless guy, sleeping in his shed out of pure sympathy, help him birth a calf?

He might be homeless, and lonelier than he'd ever been. It had been only a few months, and he'd learned life outside his cushy cocoon wasn't easy. But he still remembered his vet training. And like it or not, the poor animal needed it.

So he forced his voice to firm. "If you don't move and let me handle it, your cow will die, and you'll lose your only source of income."

A beat later, the man looked away, and Dominic took his place. He didn't bother explaining he'd finished vet school with honors, way ahead of his class. Nor that he was fully licensed to practice. What was the point, when he'd turned his back on that, and everything else?

Another set of parents lost. Another life ruined. And now, in the middle of nowhere, he still didn't feel like he belonged.

How can I belong, he thought ruefully, *when all I do is roam the land?*

With perfected movements, he dug into the cow and helped turn the foal around. Unknown to the farmer, it had gotten stuck and had he continued to pull, it would have broken the poor creature's neck – and caused the cow to bleed profusely.

As it was, Dominic had intervened in time. Minutes later, he was a bloodied mess – but the calf was slowly trying to climb on four hooves, as his mama licked him clean.

The farmer was crying tears of joy, looking up at Dominic. "How did you..."

Dominic smiled, though it felt tight to him. "Thank you for your hospitality, but I have to leave now."

He walked out of the barn, bloodied and all, grabbed his backpack and took off.

∞ ◆ ∞

It would be days before he hit another town, and it was nowhere close to what the old one was. The pickup truck he'd hitched a ride with dropped him off and Dominic headed straight to the first diner he could see.

Stomach rumbling, he took a seat at the closest table to the exit and waved the brunette waitress over. Long brown hair, pretty blue eyes, she was a sight. Not that he was interested...other than by the glint of fear in her eyes. That, he immediately noticed.

"What can I get you?"

Dominic glanced at her name plate, intrigued by her spooked posture. "Amelia, is it?"

A weak smile. Tentative. "Yeah."

What the hell have I stumbled into?

He didn't bother to look at the menu, instead passing it back to her. "I'll have whatever the house special is, and your strongest coffee."

Amelia nodded and jotted something down on her notepad. When she was done, she stole a quick glance at the corner of the room, where a beefy guy easily twice Dominic's size sat and overlooked the diner.

Dominic took note of him. He smelled like trouble – and it had nothing to do with his tattoos. Rather, there was a mean glint in his eyes, and they were glued to Amelia like a hawk.

It bothered Dominic. He'd been raised to treat women like treasures, to always put them first and respect them. Whatever the guy's relationship with Amelia was, it was none of those things. And with each minute ticking by, it bothered him more.

He shouldn't have cared. She was nothing to him.

And yet, for whatever reason, he *did* care. The wolf in him, the one he'd always been one with – even when nothing else in his life fit – rumbled his displeasure. Dominic had learned to listen to him, to let him lead when trouble was around.

Still, he kept a low profile. Sipped his coffee. Ate his food. Only once Amelia came by with the bill, did he make a move.

Dominic ignored the machine she offered for a card payment and took out his wallet, pulling out a couple bills for the meal – easily twice the required amount. He caught Amelia's hand once she reached for it and bore his cerulean blue gaze into hers, lowering his voice. "Are you okay?"

"I...." Her eyes widened and she stammered, unsure what he was asking.

Dominic turned his palm over and brought her hand to his lips, kissing it softly. He didn't mean it to seduce, though he'd seen the effect more often than not while he'd been in school. And sure enough, Amelia's lips parted, her cheeks flushing at the attention.

None of it detracted Dominic from his goal. "The man in the corner. Who is he?"

The fact Amelia didn't even look there told him more than enough. The flush disappeared off her cheeks and she paled, withdrawing her hand. "You should leave."

She turned to go, but Dominic was stubborn. "Who is he?"

Amelia searched his gaze. He pleasantly surprised by the flare of determination in her expression. She had strength, it was probably why she had survived so long. But the villain in this story was no match for her.

"You really should leave," she repeated. "He won't take well to competition."

Something akin to trepidation spread through Dominic's veins at her words. It had been a while since he'd had a proper fight. He had no interest in Amelia – rather, in removing a selfish bastard. With him gone, she'd be allowed to grow, to flower into whoever she was meant to be.

Before she could draw another breath, the man was by her side. Grabbing her waist. Pulling her into him. Dominic gritted his teeth and watched, waiting for a sign from Amelia.

"Name's Frederick," the man glared at him. "Who are you?"

Dominic caught the whiff he'd been looking for and grinned easily, leaning back in his chair. *Yep, this is going to be fucking easy.* "Your worst nightmare."

"Excuse me?"

He stood then, with one step getting in the guy's face. "You heard me."

Narrowed eyes settled on him. "Are you trying to get killed?"

Dominic shrugged, as if he couldn't be bothered. Then, he didn't hesitate. His fist slammed in Frederick's stomach with enough force to have him bend over. In the next breath, he took Amelia's hand gently and pulled her out of his grip.

Her wide eyes settled on him with both awe and fear, but Dominic only smiled tightly. "I need an answer, sweetheart, before I do anything else I might regret. Is this guy a bad man?"

She looked at him, her lower lip trembling. Then her glance fell to Frederick, and she nodded.

It was all Dominic needed to know. He grabbed the still-panting Frederick by the scruff of his shirt and dragged him outside of the diner, under the surprised looks of the other patrons eating.

They made it far away from prying eyes. Dominic had only intended to rough him up, and let him off with a warning. Teach him a lesson to treat a woman properly, so to speak. Then the damn idiot morphed right under his arm.

One moment, Dominic was holding a man captive. The next, skin turned to fur, hands to claws, and the wolf lunged at Dominic, clawing his chest.

Blood spurted from the wounds, and he hissed at the pain.

Then he saw red. A throbbing started in his temple, demanding to be loose. Dominic stood panting, fists clenched, trying to avoid the change. He'd given his wolf more freedom since they'd been away from the cities, but that didn't mean he was ready to give in with humans around.

And then Frederick lunged at him again. Dominic struck him once with his hand, and he went blasting into the trees. One last breath, and he allowed the change to overcome him.

And it was beautiful.

The change rolled over him like he was meant for it, like another parcel of his soul. His wolf wasn't taking control; he was one with Dominic. Lunging, evading, biting. Within seconds, he had the Frederick under his paws, and his jaws were at his throat, ready to deliver the justice they both understood.

"Enough."

Dominic glanced up, a growl escaping through his massive canines. Three males stood facing him, dressed in overalls and work shirts. The one who'd first spoken was at the head of their little trio. A flash of fear passed his face. "I said, enough. Release him, he is with my pack."

Dominic glared at the newcomer for another two beats, until he paled and gulped. He knew what unnerved him – his pale eyes, surrounded by a blueish tinge. His massive form, larger than most of their wolves.

That's right, dumbass. I'm a vârcolac, not a simpleton werewolf.

With a snort of satisfaction, knowing the message had gone through, Dominic stepped off Frederick.

"Thank you," the man said. "We will handle this in-pack."

Then they were gone, leaving Dominic alone. He shifted back to his human form, stole a pair of pants and shirt off a laundry line, and walked back into the diner.

Amelia finished off with her last customers and hurried to him. She took in his new clothes. "What happened? Where's Frederick?"

"He won't bother you again."

She worried her bottom lip, staring at him as if he could give her the sky and the moon, an answer to all her problems. "Who are you?"

Dominic noticed her look, sensed where she was going with it. But he wouldn't take advantage of it. Instead, he pulled her in a hug and kissed the side of her head. "No one you need to remember. You're safe now."

She breathed him in deeply. "Thank you."

Dominic pushed her away, the resolution stronger than ever. *She's not the one.*

"You will find someone to love you as you deserve, Amelia. Take care."

Then he was gone.

∞ ♦ ∞

Another day, another town. Dominic didn't mind sleeping under the stars, in fact, he chose it. Much preferred it to shady motels on the side of the road, or someone's house. There was a freedom in the nights that called to his wayward soul, and settled him into a peaceful slumber.

The next night found him walk alongside a dirt road. Something was pulling him…somewhere. Not understanding it, Dominic followed the path, stopping on and off to drink water and stretch his sore muscles.

After hours of walking, a pick-up truck pulled over. The window rolled down, and a voice called from within. "Need a ride?"

The man was old, with a wrinkled face and kind eyes. Dominic nodded. "Could do with one, thank you." He threw his bag at the back, and hopped inside the car.

"Where to?"

"As far as you're going, in that direction." Dominic pointed, more sure than ever there was something waiting for him.

Hours later, he woke up to the car stalled. "This is as far as I go, son."

Dominic looked around, surprised he'd slept so long. The scenery had completely changed. The land was wild, the mountains free… He stuck his head out the open window and breathed in deeply.

Home.

The old man chuckled. "Yeah, I thought you'd like this. You look like the type to need room to run around."

Dominic was already out the car, collecting his bag. He looked at the old man again and grinned. "Thank you."

"If you keep going onwards, there's a town a couple miles ahead. Rockland Creek, they call it. Might be of interest to you."

Dominic nodded and gave him a hundred-dollar bill for his troubles, then took off. This time, his pace was no longer slow. It was sprinting – rushing toward the ultimate destination.

∞ ♦ ∞

He was dashing between trees, playing a game with nature itself. Running. Enjoying the freedom. His wolf turned its nose up, smelling the pine trees, the water, the land...

It had been so long he'd been in such a place, simply free to return to the kind of life he's grown up with. Dominic relished it, finally free of the confines of society. There was only him, the sky and the land – and that was enough.

Then something ran smack into him, sending him tumbling into a tree, and on the ground. Dominic rose to his paws slowly, shaking his head. His eyes fell on a dirty wolf with a mangled ear. Another one popped up behind him, attacking a rusty wolf slightly larger than his own bulk.

Dominic growled, and immediately went into fight response. He picked the largest to attack, thinking the rusty wolf was the leader. Only, rather than catch him by the surprise, he was met with evasion. The other wolf dashed out of the way with practiced movements, and when Dominic tried to attack again, he growled. *Basta!*

The voice was loud in his head. Stunning enough that he paused, tilting his head to the side. *Italian?*

The rusty wolf inclined his head. *I'm not here to fight you, idiota. It's them.*

Dominic turned around then, noticing three more wolves pop out of the shadows. Four more flanked them. And then another four.

Welcome committee?

Something like that, the other wolf answered. *Get out while you can, I'll handle them.*

Dominic bristled at the order, as did his wolf. *Not likely.*

Side by side, they stalked forward, meeting the pack of wolves. They waited for the first one to jump, before splitting ranks and fighting back. Amidst all the fighting, growling, and whines of pain, something weird happened... As if by unspoken agreement, Dominic and the newcomer protected each other. They worked in tandem, dispatching the opposing wolves with scary accuracy, until they were the only two left standing.

∞ ♦ ∞

"Who the hell are you?"

The man facing him was as naked as he was, but with dark hair, onyx eyes and ruthless features. Dominic tilted his head to the side. "What were those wolves doing, attacking you?"

The stranger clenched his jaw and growled. "I asked you a question."

Dominic held his gaze, refusing to bow his head – no matter how much his instinct was telling him to do exactly that. It was the first his wolf felt like this, the first he didn't agree with it, and he refused to go against his better instincts.

Instead, he said, "As did I."

The man arched an eyebrow, and didn't look away. Onyx eyes stared into icy blue. Moments drew longer, lengthening. It was a staring contest, and there was no doubt as to its reason.

Yet when he broke the gaze, Dominic didn't do so because he'd gotten tired of it. Rather, because he'd caught that sensation again – of belonging.

Ce naiba... What the hell? He inspected their surroundings, allowing himself a frown. "What is this place?"

"My territory."

Dominics snorted and took a step closer. "Yours? What, you put your stamp on it?"

"You're welcome to fight me for it." The man grinned, as if not really believing he would.

Dominic looked at him, then the surrounding mountains. They reminded him...of home. So he smiled. "Maybe another time."

He turned to leave, but the man said, "I'm Lucas Bianchi. And those wolves attacking, they're Reapers. Seems they were here long before I arrived and, well, they tend to dislike new arrivals. I'd be careful if I was you."

Dominic nodded and left once more. It seemed like another night under the stars for him.

The next night, Dominic felt the urge for human interaction. Rockland Creek had one bar, The Cave, and it was there he went to nurse his troubles. It was no surprise when he walked in and saw Lucas at the bar, chatting up a pretty blonde. All long legs, wide smile, she was an easy catch.

And something in Dominic nagged. It wasn't the girl, per se. but he didn't like Lucas having had the upper hand earlier, as if he owned the town.

So, he waited until Lucas left to the restroom, then moved in for the girl. Suave, he propped his elbow on the bar and grinned. "Hey there."

She turned to him, and her eyes widened, lips parting. Dominic knew the look – he always took advantage of the ones that found him cute. He leaned in a bit closer. "Want to get out of here?"

"I, um," she glanced behind, to where Lucas was heading back.

Dominic looked over her head. The Italian had schooled his expression, but he could read the glare in those onyx eyes. Internally, he smirked.

"Let's dance," he pressed, and held out his hand. The girl hesitated, glanced at Lucas once more. He was only watching them, not making the least inclination to get back her attention.

So the girl shrugged, then grinned at Dominic and stepped onto the dance floor.

From there, it was only a natural conclusion they'd end up in bed. And while the romp was enjoyable, it wasn't quite as satisfying on an emotional level. Soon after she was asleep, Dominic pulled on his clothes and snuck out the fire escape.

He was barely down when a voice called out to him. "So, was she worth it?"

Dominic turned around, schooling his expression. "You're real full of yourself, aren't you?"

Lucas arched an eyebrow, but said nothing.

"What, can't handle that she picked me over you? Is that the problem, Bianchi? Big ego?" With each word, Dominic got in his face more and more.

Onyx eyes glittered with a warning. "Watch yourself, amico."

"I'm not your friend."

Lucas grinned – thinly. Then his fist was in Dominic's face – once, twice. Dominic ducked the third time, and responded with a right hook of his own. With his vârcolac strength, it was enough to push Lucas backwards – one step.

He shook his head, wiped at the corner of his mouth, then hunched his shoulders and lifted his fists. "You want a fight, country boy? Andiamo. Let's go, then!"

Dominic grinned. "Finally, we see eye to eye."

Lucas moved then with unwavering accuracy, and punched Dominic in the gut. He coughed, let out a breath, then grabbed his other hand and twisted it. Lucas surprised him by going with the flow, then pulling back at the last moment. It was a slick move – and it got Dominic off balance.

It was enough for Lucas to dig his foot into the back of his knee, forcing him to the ground. One leg. Then the other.

Dominic clenched his teeth. He had the strength to break the hold, but something in him was holding him down. His wolf. For the first time, his wolf was working against him, and there was a need to let another win.

"Submit."

"Fuck you."

Another punch, this time in the side of his ribs. Dominic hissed out in pain, but gritted his teeth rather than give in.

"I said submit, amico."

"And I said, I'm not your fucking *friend*!"

Dominic hunched over, as if he would kiss the ground. With the hold he had on him, Lucas had was forced to follow the movement. Then Dominic shrugged him off like a horse would a rider he doesn't like. Pushing off the ground, he got up at the same time Lucas did.

He wiped at his mouth, ready to continue – but Lucas was already walking away.

"If you want to stay in this town, then you'd best become my friend."

∞ ♦ ∞

It took two more nights of sleeping under the stars for Dominic to finally decide. He didn't like Lucas – hated his guts. But something told him this was the place to be, to wait for who he was meant to wait for. So who was he to fight it?

The next morning, he walked into The Cave, knowing he'd find Lucas there eating breakfast. He took a seat opposite him. Lucas didn't even glance up.

"Fine," Dominic said through gritted teeth. "I'm listening."

Lucas met his glare, but took his time speaking. First, he dabbed a napkin around his lips, following by taking a leisurely slow sip of his coffee. Finally, he said, "You're a wolf. I'm a wolf. And the Reapers in this town don't like newcomers. My proposal is simple: have my back, and I'll have yours."

"So, what, be in your pack?"

"And work for me," Lucas grinned. "I'm opening up a mechanic shop."

Dominic looked pointedly at his fine hands. "You don't look like a mechanic."

"I know cars."

"So do I."

Lucas narrowed his eyes. "Then work for me."

It was not a suggestion, but a demand. Dominic had no doubts about the tone, or the feeling behind it. And still, he leaned back in the booth, toyed with a napkin. Chewed the side of his cheek.

Dominic waited a beat, then two, before voicing the one word they both knew he'd already spoken. 'Fine."

∞ ◆ ∞

Always waiting. Always wondering. *Is she out there? Will I find her?*

It was a need, burning inside him with each passing day. But it would be ages later… Long after Lucas opened his mechanic shop. Long after two more joined their ranks. And much, much longer after…

It would be then he'd walk down the street one day, having all but lost hope, and a bus would pull up in town. And his wolf would freeze, demanding his attention. And he'd look up to curls the color of flames, eyes of the deepest forest, filled with vulnerability – and something else.

And he'd know, then and there, that he'd found his one. Dominic was finally home.

Turn to page 101 for a preview

of Dominic's story!

∞ ∞ ∞

A TWISTED CASE

-Finn

"So.... Will you take the case, then?"

The dark-haired lawyer behind the desk looked up from his notes. A slight frown creased his forehead, giving his youthful face an otherwise severe look. His deep emerald eyes glittered with warning, though his smile was soft. "What made you think I wouldn't?"

Head bowed, the client fiddled with the hat in his hand and stuttered, "Nothing, just…" He paused, unable – or unwilling – to go on. The rest of the confession came out in a whisper. "Everyone else refused when they saw the name of the defendant. I thought you would, too."

"You thought wrong." Another smile, this time to take the bite out of his words.

The client stared at the run-down carpet, clutching the woolen hat in his hands. "I'm a simple man, sir. But, thank you. Thank you from the bottom of my heart. For my kids, and my wife…" A sob clogged his throat, and he stopped talking again.

By the time he looked up, the lawyer was holding out his hand for him to shake. "Let's take this bastard down, once and for all."

Trembling, the client took the offered hand, and a deal was struck.

∞ ♦ ∞

Later that evening, Finn McConnell stared out the foggy window of his office. The city at his feet was buzzing with noise, as it always was. The human part of him wanted to mix with others, interact and enjoy life with his kin. Yet the darker part, the primal part, knew it was but a wishful intention.

He had willfully chosen this path. Being a solicitor, taking pro bono cases, didn't meant a lot of money, but it did mean justice was served. And Finn craved the rules, cared to make them respected.

As if a reminder, his landline rang. Once, twice. Finn waited for the third ring, and it never came. Satisfied with the signal, he opened a small drawer and pulled out a faded-looking cellphone. Pressing a key, he waited as it speed-dialed the pre-programmed number to another burner phone. "What is it, Ronan? I'm in the middle of a case."

"The pack needs to meet tonight, boss. Brian found his mate, and you need to approve it."

Finn let out a chuckle, turning to glance out the window of his office. It had been a while since he'd witnessed the oaths of mating between two of his pack. He'd been gone too long… "Eager, is he?"

A booming laugh resounded on the other line. "That's my little brother, mate. He's *always* eager."

Rolling his eyes, Finn nodded to his reflection. "Call it, but make it before sunrise. And do me a favor, will you? Instruct them both on what goes on. I don't want to have to explain hand-fasting to some pups again."

Another laugh, then Ronan hung up. Finn went back to staring at his reflection. Why wasn't he with his pack, leading them? Another alpha would have. Instead, he was kilometers away – towns away, even. Fighting for a legal justice that only humans cared about. He couldn't have both worlds, the human and the wolf. And yet he still tried. Because justice mattered, and rules mattered most of all.

Blinking at his reflection, Finn thought back to his client from earlier. It was a sad reminder that justice didn't matter to all. Niall Walsh had lost his wife to the negligence of a tycoon. It could have been avoided – *should have* been avoided. But it hadn't, and now he was left raising three kids on his own, and mourning an innocent, but much dead, wife.

His mirrored image taunted him with what he'd face in court. The best of the best solicitors, those the money could buy, and who would sell their soul to the devil. They already had, in many ways. As for Finn... At only twenty-six, he was cynical, but still an idealist. He didn't wear expensive suits, didn't flaunt jewelry he didn't have. His brains were his best asset – as was his ability to taste a jury's emotions before they even could. But that was a facet of his personality he didn't let many see.

A buzz by the desk drew his gaze to his regular cellphone. A pretty blonde's laughing image taunted him with promises of wild nights, but he ignored the call. There was no room for desire in his mind tonight, only for justice. Setting the phone to silent mode, Finn picked up the binder with his notes from earlier.

Ciaran Loughey. A tycoon, owner of a chain of jewelry stores, he had money, fame, a family when it was convenient. He was backed up by most politicians and upper echelon of society, because their pockets were lined with his blood money. And it seemed his greed had no limit. It had been his excessive stinginess that had led to a cheap security system, and one of his stores being robbed.

Finn had written testimonies from two employees who confirmed having raised the issue of security with their managers, and those above them. One had even written to Ciaran himself – and had proof of delivery for the letter. And still, the store had been robbed, an employee – Niall's wife – had died, and now the insurance refused to pay out. Rumors flew that Ciaran didn't have the right security in place, and he'd threatened Niall himself with a lawsuit if he opened his mouth to confirm them.

Which had opened the door for a lawsuit. Gross negligence manslaughter. And Finn wasn't used to taking prisoners. He intended to make the man suffer. After all, his selfish decision had caused a woman's death, and her husband and three sons were now left bereft.

No, this won't do at all, Finn thought as he shrugged off his blazer, tore the shirt off him, and leaned back in the chair.

His wolf tended to react in temperature spikes, and now was no different. The cool air helped his heated skin, lowering the temperature of his primal self. A massive drawback of being away from his pack was difficulty with controlling him – especially when he was ready to kill.

It's going to be a long few nights.

∞ ♦ ∞

Finn knew the moment he stepped into the courtroom that something was wrong. It was deserted, except for one man seated in the defense panel. Dark-haired like Finn, but dressed in an impeccable suit, he didn't glance up from the phone in his hand. Scowling, he scrolled through the electronic keyboard as if riveted by the tiny words.

It wasn't his silence that bothered him. Finn had recognized his profile from the media pictures – this was Ciaran himself. He'd expected the man to be morose and snobby. So no, the silence didn't bother him, but *something* did. Finn couldn't put his finger on it right off the bat, so he headed to the prosecution side.

Setting down his worn briefcase, he opened it and took out a few papers. The meeting with the judge was meant to confirm whether the case would go to trial or not.

"You think you have a chance against me, mate?"

At the sound of his smooth, yet ruthless voice, Finn looked up at the man for the first time. And then it hit him – he tasted nothing in the air, not even anger. No emotions whatsoever. Only a coldness that got to his bones.

"What?"

Ciaran finally looked up, and his golden eyes glared back. "I *will* win."

Finn tried not to let his confidence get to him, but already his wolf was rumbling in disapproval. "Ciaran, I suppose."

A slight narrowing of the eyes. "Do you not know who you've dragged in this court?"

Finn only smirked and went back to his papers. A shuffle in the air raked him the wrong way, and he caught taste of…ashes. He glanced up, trying to determine where the change had come from. Only instead of emotionless golden eyes, he now looked into fiery flames.

The chill in his bones intensified, and only one word passed Finn's numb lips as he stumbled back a few meters. "*Dragan!*"

Ciaran smiled – cold as ice. "Aye, you finally get it."

The doors opened, and Ciaran went back to his phone. People started shuffling in while Finn tried to focus back on his notes. The man was part of a destroyed race, and if he was what Finn thought he was – a dragon – that meant his entire clan was...

"Feckin' hell."

"What was that?" Niall had joined him, and looked up fearfully.

Finn gritted his teeth and shook his head. *This changes nothing,* he told himself. *I'll get him, one way or another.*

∞ ♦ ∞

ALEXA WHITEWOLF

"What's got you so riled up?"

Finn turned from the window to face the newcomer. Ronan strolled into his office, glancing at the mess of papers and things thrown everywhere.

"A case." He tapped the wooden desk, more in an effort to collect himself. Ronan's hesitation and trepidation coated the air, making it hard to focus on the task at hand. "What is it?"

Rather than answer, Ronan picked up a stack of papers. His eyebrows shot way up when he noticed one of the names. "Ciaran Loughey?" He met Finn's gaze. "What the hell did you get involved in?"

Finn dropped into the chair, pinching the bridge of his nose. "A bloody mess, that's what."

"Why the face? You've got a pack, boss. Put us to use."

Sighing, Finn told him about the case. When he got to the meeting at the court, Ronan whistled low. "He's got some nerve. And a dragan? I thought their race was all but gone."

"Apparently, it was just my luck to run into one."

"More like antagonize him," Ronan snorted. He rubbed his chin, then said, "What about the judge? What's your feel?"

"He sympathizes. But one look at Ciaran had him freeze multiple times. I'm not sure he can see this through, let alone sentence the head of a dragon clan."

"You think he knows?"

Finn thought back to the judge's innate fearful response. "Nah, more that he perceives the danger in opposing someone like Ciaran."

Ronan was quiet for a moment, then said, "But you've got it in the bag. The witnesses, the paper trail... What more do you need?"

Finn groaned. "I need Ciaran nailed. Proof that he knew what he was doing in picking the cheapest security company. If I have it on paper that he was offered options and purposefully chose the least expensive, it would change the game."

Ronan shrugged, "So, we'll get it. I'll take a few of the guys and dig into it."

Finn shook his head. "It's too dangerous. I don't want the pack involved in this."

"Boss, no offense, but we're already involved. You may keep your distance from us, hunting justice for humans, but whatever you throw your strength behind drags all of us in it. And you chose to dig your heels into this, so now we need to stick by you."

Knowing it was true, Finn nodded. The invisible burden on his shoulders got heavier with the movement. "Fine. But keep your distance from his men, make sure you're not seen, and I need to know of any developments. As soon as they happen."

"You got it." Ronan got up to head out, but Finn called out.

"What had you so hesitating earlier?"

"I hate it when you do that," Ronan muttered under his breath. A faint smile graced his lips – something not easily seen. "If you must know, I met someone. And I'd like you to meet her, too."

Finn laughed. "After this mess is over, it's a deal."

"I'll hold you to that."

Ronan walked out then. As he watched his friend and beta leave, Finn got an odd feeling in the pit of his stomach – like he wouldn't be seeing him again.

∞ ♦ ∞

There is no worse omen than a phone ringing in the middle of the night. Even more so when it won't stop ringing.

Groaning and swearing under his breath, Finn picked up. "Yeah?"

"I didn't know who else to call."

Finn froze, then jumped out of bed and pulled on a pair of sweatpants and a shirt. Within moments, he was flooring his old car through the half-asleep city. When he got to the neighborhood, police were already on site. A younger-looking cop headed towards him to warn him off, but Finn growled. "I'm his solicitor. Let me the fuck in."

The man hesitated, but an older police officer moved forward. "He's good, I know him. Let him through." Finn ducked under the yellow tape, and scowled at the young policeman.

He was a young punk, probably still a rookie, and untrained in the ways of their world. Plus, he was human. The older one knew the drill, and that alone earned him a nod of respect from Finn. It was good having wolves in various professions.

Inside the house, Finn took stock of the broken living room window, and the three kids in a corner. A policewoman was speaking softly to them, and they seemed to be sipping cups of tea. Niall was on a couch, holding a pack of ice to his head. A nasty bruise was forming, and Finn saw a towel filled with blood tossed on the ground.

The two cops interrogating him looked up as he entered. "I'm Finn McConnell," he said, dropping a hand on Niall's shoulder. "What happened?"

"Earlier this evening, your client was attacked. He didn't report it. Within moments of getting home, a brick was tossed through his window, resulting in these damages." A pause. "He still won't talk."

Finn narrowed his eyes on the cops. "Maybe if you'd give him a minute to catch his breath, he would. Leave us."

The eldest of the cops opened his mouth to say something. Finn narrowed his eyes, letting enough of his anger seep loose. He knew what the humans would perceive – an innate reaction, telling them to back the fuck off.

It was one thing to taste emotions in the air, but his were always well kept under wraps. Unless something took him by surprise – and whatever this was, it wasn't good news.

After a hesitation, the cops headed into the hall, leaving him alone with his client. Heart pounding, Finn knelt before Niall. "What happened?"

Tears filled the man's eyes, and his fear and despair permeated the air. "It's Ciaran. One of his goons from the courthouse, he followed me. I recognized him, and he was the one who attacked me. Probably the same one who threw the brick."

Finn glanced at the cops. "And why didn't you tell them?"

"I can't. He'll kill me. You know as well as I do that it's a warning. I won't leave my kids orphaned."

Finn inhaled sharply, trying to hold his anger at bay. "He won't get to do anything, I swear it."

"How can you be sure? Ciaran… He's not like you. There's something wrong with him."

Finn gave a short laugh. "Yeah, there's something wrong with him, alright. And I plan on fixing it."

He stood and walked to the cops. "My client won't speak as to who hurt him. However, if you want to dig deeper, feel free. He's currently involved in a lawsuit with a rather powerful man. Three guesses who's leading this witness intimidation scheme."

Ignoring their startled looks, Finn walked out. One glance at the older cop from earlier, and he followed in his footsteps. When they were far enough from the house, Finn stopped and took out a lighter. He didn't smoke – hadn't since he'd been a boy. But playing with the flame calmed him down. A deep breath later, he spoke out of the corner of his mouth. "I want uniforms around his house, protecting him and his kids. I don't care how, but arrange it."

The man nodded. "Who do we have to look out for?"

Finn glanced at the darkening clouds. "The skies. Be wary of the damn skies." With an equally darkening expression, he growled. "Ciaran Loughey is on his last straw."

∞ ♦ ∞

The trial went on. And on.

First the employees refused to testify. Then the witnesses disappeared.

In the end, the judge had no chance but to declare Ciaran cleared of all charges. The smug bastard walked off as Finn's client collapsed into sobs. Finn tasted Niall's defeat, his unbearable misery, and could do nothing to console him. The man responsible for his wife's death had just walked off free – there was nothing to be done.

Still, he glared after Ciaran. At the entrance of the courtroom, the dragan turned around and smirked. His look told Finn he wasn't quite done.

∞ ♦ ∞

The same evening, Finn was woken up yet again in the middle of the night. Only, it wasn't due to his cellphone. A sense of loss, of unbearable agony spread through his body. He gasped, panting and sweating in bed, waiting for it to go away. When it finally did – interminable seconds later – a body-numbing cold took over him.

Finn grappled out of bed, searching for clothes. His hand encountered a phone in the darkness, and he dialed Ronan's number. Despite the distance, he'd always been attuned to his wolves, especially his beta. And something was telling him now it was imperative to contact Ronan. But the line rang on, and on.

Dread filling the pit of his stomach, Finn pulled on clothes and once more got into his car. The scene felt all too familiar when he sped down the streets, heart in the pit of his stomach, but he tried not to let panic overrule him.

At least until he got to Ronan's out-of-town bungalow, at the cul-de-sac of a tiny residential address… And found ashes. There was nothing left of the house, only a pile of bricks, amd broken ruins of what used to be a home.

"Ronan…"

Finn left the car running in the middle of the road and stumbled out. The dread in his gut intensified. He tasted ashes, but also anger – not his. An alien anger. A dragan. His eyes searched the skies, and he could have sworn seeing a shadow pass, hiding behind clouds.

"Ciaran, you feckin' piece of shite!"

A roar of pain burst from his throat, and he fell to the ground, hitting it with unleashed fury until his knuckles were bloodied, the skin hanging off them.

How had the humans not seen it?

How had Ronan not escaped?

And worst of all… Why had he, the alpha, not been around to prevent this from ever taking place?

Guilt bubbled up his throat, escaping into another roar. "RONAN!!!!!!" It ended on a howl, scorching his insides, echoing around. Lights turned on in the few houses surrounding the area.

Before any residents could see him, a shudder ran through Finn, and he was no longer human. White paws dusted with grey covered the ground, a black nose dug deep into the rubbles, searching, questing, praying to find no trace of his friend.

But Ronan was there. His charred body was unmistakable, a familiar pewter necklace still hanging around his neck. Finn vowed then and there that his friend's death would not go unavenged.

Robotically, Finn made his way to his office. He pulled up all the files on Ciaran, all the research. Downing cup after cup of coffee, he poured over the documents, searching. Seeing if anything could be done. His family called too many times to count.

Word must have spread of Ronan's death. He had decisions to make – a new beta to choose.

The pain was too fresh, the agony too raw. He refused to speak to anyone and turned both phones off, even unhooked the landline.

And then the news caught his attention. Police in front of a beaten down house, three kids crying at the front. The area was familiar, though it took him a second to realize why. When he did, Finn's throat clogged up. "No..."

It was Niall's house. And according to the news anchor, he'd committed suicide following the verdict.

Finn grabbed his coat and drove like hell to his former client's neighborhood. The cop he'd spoken to, the one who assured him Niall would be protected, was on duty. He saw Finn approaching and shook his head. Regret was etched all over his face.

"We had him, but following the verdict the guys eased up, tried to let him get back to his life..." The rest faded away as Finn walked away. They were excuses he did not want to hear.

In the house, Finn only had to step one foot inside before he tasted it – the fiery anger that had been missing at the trial. *This was no suicide.*

Fists clenched, he stomped out of the house, slamming the door. A growl of agony left him and he hit the closest thing – his car. A deep breath, then he forced the red haze clouding him back, and got inside. He drummed his fingers on the steering wheel for a beat, before putting the car into gear. The time for thinking was over. As was the time for the human legal system to act.

It was time for *his* justice.

And he knew just where to find Ciaran.

∞ ♦ ∞

The club was open all night long. It should be – Ciaran owned it, too. Finn gained entrance with a few well-placed bills, and took stock in the darkest corner of the bar. He was overrun with anger, regret – he should have done more, *could have* done more. Had he not been confined by stupid rules.

Rules he'd chosen to follow.

But there were no rules now. Only him, Ciaran, and justice in sight. When he was done playing around with girl after girl, the dragan left behind his security detail and went outside.

Finn followed from afar, keeping his footsteps light. Ciaran was walking, stumbling, uncaring. The minute he ducked into an alley to relieve himself, Finn went after him. Without hesitation, he grabbed him by the neck, smashing his face against the brick wall.

A crack echoed in the air, and Ciaran cursed under his breath. Hands to his bloody nose, he turned to Finn. His eyes flashed to flames in the darkness. "Do you have a death wish, *faoladh*?"

"Aye, maybe I do." Finn ducked his punch and went for his gut. "Or maybe I just want to taste your blood."

Ciaran drunkenly tried to hit again, but Finn knew his enemy. He'd studied him the last few weeks. Dragans had a thirst for gold, for vices, and it was their weakness. Alcohol and drugs, they relished, but both inhibited their ability to shift, let alone keep a handle on their powers.

In short, Ciaran was vulnerable. And he was alone. So, Finn ducked and punched again, this time hitting him under the jaw. Ciaran's back hit the side of a dumpster, and slid to the ground. But Finn wasn't done. He picked him up by his shirt and hit again. And again.

A red haze filled his sight. Ronan. Niall. Three poor kids who were now orphans. Ronan's girl who would never know the joy of having a mate. Brian, who'd lost a brother. His fist was numb from the hits, but still he went at it.

By the time he was done, Ciaran was on the ground, his face an unrecognizable mess. It would take hours for it to heal – if it ever did. Still, the dragan looked up at him through one swollen eye. "You've signed your death warrant."

"Maybe so," Finn growled, towering over him. "But at least you'll lose your clan over this."

A dragan chief who got beat up? It was bound to lead to a fight for alpha. And, if nothing else, that meant Ciaran would lose *something* from the entire mess.

Finn spit at his feet, then walked away. For the first time that night, he slept peacefully – aided by the good contents of a whiskey bottle.

Retaliation was swift. The following morning, his office was trashed. Over the next few weeks, clients started being threatened. But it was only the build up to the final nail in the coffin.

One night Finn parked the car in front of his house. He didn't even make it to his front door before a group attacked him. When they were done and he was on the ground, coughing up blood, Ciaran walked up to him.

He was wearing an impeccable suit once more, not a hair out of place. His beatings had healed, too. Arching an eyebrow, the dragan smirked. "Lose my pack, you said? It's you who will lose yours. You have a choice: death to all your kin, or exile. And let me never see your face, faoladh, ever again."

∞ ♦ ∞

It took him an hour, but finally Finn was able to move off the grass. He crawled back into the car, resting his head on the steering wheel. He fought to catch his breath, but each inhalation increased his agony.

"I've fucked up."

The whisper was loud in the small space, its only competition his ragged breath. Finn looked at the icy moon, visible from his spot. "What the hell do I do, Ronan?"

There was no answer, but deep down, he knew his next step. Men like Ciaran didn't give up. His rage had led him to break the rules, and now he had to pay the price.

Starting the car, he drove out of town, coughing blood all the way. He was heading to the one place he should have when all this mess had started. When he pulled in the driveway, just as the sun poked over the horizon, two men stepped out of the house. His brother and cousin greeted him, their similar green eyes looking him over in concern. They caught him as he stumbled out of the car, holding his weight up.

"Call a pack meet," Finn whispered, before passing out.

When he came to, whispered voices surrounded him.

"Is it true?"

"Is the dragan's clan after us?"

"He must have pissed them off."

"Don't talk about him like that. He's our alpha."

"And how can he protect us, if he can't even protect himself? Ronan died because of him!"

Finn coughed and opened his eyes. He was surrounded by his family, and as much of the pack that fit in the cramped living room. "You're right," he hoarsely. "I'm here to pick a replacement."

∞ ♦ ∞

We'll miss you.

Finn glanced at his cellphone one more time. The text made his heart clench, but he knew it was for the best. Choosing someone to take his place had been easy – his brother was the natural pick. He was strong enough to keep Ciaran from coming after his pack, and it was for the best.

Leaving was another matter. Ireland was his in his very bones, and the thought of never returning left him empty, bereft. Even if it was the only choice, it wasn't the easiest to make.

His flight was called. Holding his ribs, Finn shuffled to the plane. Each step was harder, and every muscle in his body wanted to rebel against the act.

He wasn't leaving because he feared for himself – but for his pack, for their sake. If he stayed, it would mean certain death, and he already had two such deaths on his consciousness.

One last glance over his shoulder. The rolling emerald hills taunted him. Clouds hid the sun, but he already missed the wet smell of the outside. Memories of another time, a simpler time, shifted through his mind. Tears pricked at the corner of his eyes – tears of rage – but he blinked them away.

Resolutely, he turned around and handed the hostess his passport.

Maybe an ocean will be enough for Ciaran. Maybe one day I'll come back home. Maybe…it's not forever. Just for right now.

That last bit of hope gave him the courage to move onwards. Head held high, he turned his back on Ireland and stepped on the plane.

Turn to page 139 for a preview

of Finn's story!

∞ ∞ ∞

A NEW HOME

-Tristan

"WATCH OUT!"

His roar got lost in ashes and blaze. Another explosion rang nearby – too close. Tristan crouched to the ground, trying to stay out of the line of fire without losing sight of the combatants.

I need higher ground, he thought.

A quick glance around confirmed no one could see him. His fellow soldiers were taking heavy fire from snipers set up above buildings. Their mission had been simple – extract some information from a confidential informant. Only, it seemed to have been an ambush or their communications had been intercepted. Either way, Tristan had found himself outmanned, outgunned, and quickly separated from his peers.

Only one way out of this.

He hated taking chances, but if he wanted to survive, he had to. And though Tristan didn't have anyone to return to back home – not anymore, at least – he still preferred to live. So he ducked behind a Jeep and shed his clothes, dropping the two guns he'd confiscated off his attackers on the ground.

Then he crouched low, low... And let his wolf out.

The change came over him in a wave, leaving him shuddering and gasping. Then he was wolf, blending with the darkness. His ashy coat made for great camouflage in the darkness, but still he focused on his paws, trying to lower his bulk. On a regular day, he was the size of a small bear, and it would make him too easy a target.

Finally, content with his size, he picked up the two weapons in his mouth and trotted into the distance. Into a building. Up some stairs. A glance around confirmed he was alone, and he shifted back to human.

Naked, Tristan lowered himself onto the dusty ground and hoisted the weapon, taking aim. *Perfect line of sight.* Snip. Snip. Snip.

Bullets whizzed out of the gun, hitting each target in turn. The fight was done before it was truly started.

∞ ♦ ∞

"A commendation, huh?" His buddy, Ash, grinned and lifted his tainted whiskey glass. "Good on you, Tris."

Tristan rolled his eyes, then took a big gulp of a plastic cup. "Not like I did much. Shouldn't be this big a deal."

Ash gave him a look. "Are you serious right now? We walked into an ambush. I know your Brazilian blood's got you cool as a cucumber, but we would've all been dead if you hadn't managed to get high ground and cover us." His voice got hoarser with emotion. "Make no mistake, Tristan. It's well deserved and all the guys will back me up on this."

Tristan looked to his drink, scratching the back of his head. Uncomfortable was an understatement for how he felt. No one in his unit knew what he was – what he could do. It was probably best that way. Yet it also made for moments like these, where he didn't really feel like the praise was deserved.

A rookie walked in, meeting his gaze nervously. "The CO wants to see you, sir."

Tristan nodded and stood. Straightening his clothes, he downed the rest of his drink, then swished some water in his mouth and spit. Before leaving the tent, he arched an eyebrow at Ash. "Oy, meu amigo? Leave the kid alone, dumbass."

Ash tended to get snippy with rookies. He took too much pleasure torturing them. His reasoning was that they needed to toughen up. And while Tristan technically agreed, after that evening's events, he felt they'd all deserved some leeway.

The commanding officer's tent was nothing compared to the man standing in the middle. Tall, broad of shoulders, head shaved, he was imposing. When he turned, the CO's blue eyes were icy, though a smile tugged at his lips.

"Tristan Cayne, is it?"

"Yes, sir!" Tristan saluted.

After a beat, an extra hard stare, the CO nodded. "At ease, soldier."

Tristan didn't relax. He never could, not around a superior. But he did allow himself a breath as he waited to be spoken to.

"How old are you, son?"

"Twenty-three, sir."

Another nod, more speculative than anything. "By the by, the name's Blake, not 'sir'." Ignoring Tristan's stunned expression, he continued, "What you did today is admirable. A lesser man might not have pulled it off."

Silence extended between them, with Tristan struggling to find a reason for the meeting – and failing. Just as he was about to break protocol and ask, Blake said, "Then again, you're no man, are you?"

Tristan's jaw went slack. "Como..." He caught himself from entering into his native tongue, and instead tried again. "How did you find out?"

Blake grinned, for real this time. "I knew it since the beginning, son. I was waiting to see if you'd pick up on mine."

Tristan couldn't help narrowing his eyes. "Yours, sir?"

The CO stared at him for a long moment. Something shifted in the air, an impenetrable quality that once it hit Tristan's nose, had him take a step back. His eyes went wide as he picked up a scent that hadn't been there before. "What the..."

"That's me, son. Also a wolf."

"Mas.. And you can mask your scent?"

"Bet your ass I can."

"Why tell me all this?"

"I want you to come work with me."

Tristan frowned. "All due respect, but I already do, sir."

"No, son. I'm putting together a new unit. There are creatures in the night that no one can fight, and someone has to. We'll be it."

A chance to be free, to be who he was meant to be? Tristan didn't hesitate. "Where do I sign up?"

Blake's satisfied expression answered before his words registered. "You just did."

∞ ♦ ∞

Cold air hit his skin. A frigid wind had picked up and was getting worse. Tristan huddled deeper into his coat. He'd never been cold in his life, but this was new. It had been hell since the chopper had dropped them in smack middle of Siberia. That had been a week earlier. Blake hadn't said what they were hunting, only that they'd be briefed closer to the town.

Tristan still waited. He breathed in again, feeling the bitter air burn through his insides. Mutters around him made him chuckle under his breath. Blake had recruited some rookies too – more wolves – and they weren't too happy about being yanked to some cold-ass place.

Then the air around him shifted and he stopped laughing. His ears perked, and though he didn't move, he tried to figure out what the hell he'd picked up on.

The glow caught his attention first, over by a tree. When Tristan looked that way, the woman's beauty struck him dumb. Long, flowing blonde hair to her waist. Beautiful blue eyes, features as sharp as a princess. She smiled, and he thought he saw a hint of fangs, but was too focused on her blood red lips.

One pale hand encased in silk lifted up to summon him, and he didn't hesitate. Got to his feet, forgetting about his watching post. All he cared about was getting closer to her.

With each crunch of the snow, he inched nearer. Her body was shimmering under the white gown, and her eyes flashed in anticipation.

"Come to me, yes..." The words were spoken in another language, but he knew their meaning.

And then he was there and she was touching his cheek, moving his chin to the side. And Tristan couldn't move... Smelling her sugary fragrance... And then something else. Something deeper. A rotting scent.

He tried to pull back, but she was strong. Then a whizz went through the air, and she slackened against him. A second later, she fell to the snow, and curled into herself like paper burning.

Mere moments later, only a wooden stake was left of her. He blinked and glanced around. His eyes landed on Blake, who was panting. He'd been the one to throw the stake.

"Congratulations, son. You found our target."

Tristan looked back at what remained of the bundle. "Puta merda... What *was* that?"

"Something better suited for Hell. Fancy a fire?"

∞ ♦ ∞

"They're coming!"

Tristan was up in an instant, Blake's voice being the wake-up call. Humidity filled the air, and he was already covered in sweat. They were deep in the Amazonian jungle this time, hunting a type of shifter that had taken to cannibalism.

Shaking sleep out of his eyes, Tristan grabbed the hunting knife by his side. This time, he wouldn't be taken unawares. He glanced around, noticing his fellow soldiers crouched, ready to strike. Each one had similar knives in their hands and mirroring expressions of determination.

Human weapons were no use against these creatures – but sterling silver was. So Tristan crouched under the bush, blending in with his camouflage, barely breathing, waiting for the first one. When the bear-like thing passed through, Tristan jumped on its back. Undaunted by its massive size – easily twice his – he dug the knife through fur and hardened skin. A howl more human than animal tore from the creature's throat. Similar ones echoed all around, as more bears were attacked by Tristan's pack.

Then the animal under him shook him off, trampled on him. Tristan landed on his back – hard. In the next breath, he was rolling over, switching to wolf and attacking the bear full on. There was only way the fight would end – to the death.

Later, filled with blood, he discarded the corpse and shuffled to his commander. Blake was busy cleaning his knife on a carcass.

A shadow moved from the corner of his eye, and Tristan stopped in his tracks. Hidden in the bushes was a child. No more than six or seven years old, he had long hair and was only wearing some kind of animal skin wrapped around his lower body. But it wasn't his appearance that struck Tristan, rather, it was his eyes. They were filled with sorrow, tears streaming down his cheeks, as he looked upon the battle scene and held back his cries.

When he noticed Tristan staring at him, he took a step back. That, more than anything, made the soldier realize the truth. The bears he'd helped kill.... they were the child's kin. Not mindless creatures, after all.

"Cayne, you coming?"

He glanced away for a second at the shout. By the time he looked back, the young boy was gone.

It was with a heavy heart that Tristan headed closer. The adrenaline of the battle was gone, as was the satisfaction of having rid the world of evil. Because how could they, when they'd caused that much pain to someone so innocent?

And still, when he met Blake's firm gaze and unwavering belief in the mission, Tristan's doubts washed away. "What's next, sir?"

"Hungary."

∞ ♦ ∞

Days turned into weeks. Weeks into months. Soon, a year had passed since Tristan had entered Blake's special unit. They'd been through countless countries, some remote, others full front and center of the action. They'd crossed every continent, every ocean, and still there was no lack of creatures to kill. Blake had informants and wherever they were called, they went. In time, the ten soldiers they had originally left with trimmed down to seven, then five. All killed in action.

At night, Tristan thought of those fallen comrades. Of their families waiting back home, about to get the obligatory visit from the service men. What would they be told? Some bullshit excuse that they'd served their country. But was it really true? Nothing they did was sanctioned from higher up. No one wanted to be aware of just how inconsequential human leaders were, when the rest of the world was populated by creatures of nightmares. And in the end, did it really matter? If the families knew the true story behind the deaths of their loved ones, would it truly help the pain?

Though he wasn't in charge of the men, Tristan felt each and every one of their losses. Their shouts of agony kept him up at night, and their spirits always felt like they were surrounding him.

And lately, it was more than that. More than the soldiers' shouts. He dreamed of the creatures they killed. Feared them. Dreaded them. And sometimes pitied them. Months had passed and still he remembered that little boy in the jungle, and wondered if he'd survived on his own.

One such night, as he was going through a bottle of cheap scotch trying to make himself sleepy, Blake came by.

"You'll want to go easy on that, son. Big day tomorrow."

Tristan glanced at him out of the corner of his eye. "Não... I'll be fine."

"I've no doubt about it. You never failed me. But you should watch yourself nonetheless."

Tristan looked at the bottle, then took a big swig. He purposefully avoided looking at his commander, for fear of what he'd see in his expression. But when Blake turned as if about to leave, he called out to him. "Espera... Wait. What...What happens to them?"

A silence. "Who?"

"The families of the men who die with us."

A sharp inhale was his response, followed by a long sigh. "Is that what's keeping you up at night?"

"Talvez..." Maybe.

Blake sat next to him and held out his hand. It took Tristan a moment to realize he was asking for the drink. Once the commander had a swig, he passed the bottle back to Tristan.

"Nasty stuff, that."

Tristan shrugged. "They call it țuică here. Some kind of Romanian vodka." He hesitated, then pressed his earlier point. "The families, sir?"

"Yeah, they keep me up at night, too. There's no easy answer, son. They're informed of the death, not of the circumstances. I've ensured the pension of each soldier is topped off with a sizeable anonymous donation that will ensure their financial ease, at least. But it's nothing compared to the emotional scar of having someone never come back."

Something in his tone made Tristan's ears perk. "Do you have family waiting for you, sir?"

A bitter laugh. "A while back, I did. Then the wife left. And my son.... He's the reason I'm doing this to begin with."

Another swig of alcohol. "He served, too, you see. And after a tour, he was ready to come back home with only a concussion. Then the makeshift hospital he was in was attacked in the middle of the night by bloodthirsty demons. No one was prepared. My son protected the humans, put his life on the line, and died doing so. Without him, they didn't stand a chance. It was a massacre, all caught on video." Another pause. Another swig. "So the day I buried him, I made a promise to myself. That no other father will know that pain so long as I'm alive. And I know I can't catch them all... but the more I do catch, the easier it gets, and the safer it'll be."

Tristan weighed his words. "And you never doubt that what we're doing is wrong? That maybe by hunting all these creatures, we're creating more?"

The colonel laughed. "You've had too much of this, son." He stood and walked away. Before entering the tent, he whispered, "I never doubt. Because in this world, to doubt is to open yourself up to weakness. And the mission is too important."

Tristan stayed gazing at the mountains a bit longer, until his eyes were playing tricks on him and he was seeing things where there were only shadows. Finally, he went to sleep.

∞ ♦ ∞

"Wake up, soldier."

Tristan got up, blinking. It couldn't have been longer than a few hours since he'd fallen asleep. His CO was standing over him, hand on his gun, glancing around.

"Que… What's going on?" Tristan jumped to his feet, eyes seeking danger.

"We've been made. And there's another problem, another incident taking place a couple countries down. I got the call this morning. We need to head over to Greece."

"What about the vârcolaci around here?"

The CO scowled. "Not as big of a priority as what's home."

"Greece, you mean?" When he nodded, Tristan pressed, "What is it?"

"Something way worse than some Romanian wolves running rogue."

Less than an hour later, a car came to pick them up in the mountains and drove them to a small field where a plane was waiting. Then they were up in the air, heading for another mission.

In Greece, they landed outside a tiny village, way off the map. Tristan didn't know his way around, but Blake was home. He joked around with locals, and even as they passed through seemed to belong. Since night was coming and they couldn't room with the humans, the CO gave orders to sleep under the starry skies. Still exhausted from many restless nights, Tristan passed out on the soft grass.

It was the smell that woke him up, though he would forever blame himself for not hearing the villagers cries in the night. But the smell... Charred flesh, rotten corpses, and death itself. Gagging, Tristan woke up and immediately knew something was wrong. The rest of his unit was asleep. He jostled them up, then didn't waste time. Grabbed his gun and crouched into town.

They were everywhere. Larger than dogs, with black, matted fur and yellow eyes. One seemed to lead them, with a white line of fur on his chest. Tristan tried to aim for him, but missed. Instead the creatures turned to him. No matter how many bullets he fired, he couldn't kill them.

One in particular was heading for him, its head bowed low, beady yellow eyes tinged with red intent on him. Tristan saw his life flash before his eyes. Just as the creature lunged, someone moved from the side. A wooden stake was driven in the creature's chest. And Tristan stared in awe at the old man who had done it. He caught him as he fell, but he could do nothing to help him. His weary eyes met Tristan's and he whispered one word, "Vrykolakas..."

Growls to the side drew his attention. Tristan moved the old man off him and grabbed the stake. The creature was dead, but too many were around. He heard bullets whizz past him and turned to his men. "Stakes! Forget the bullets, use your stakes!"

Then he joined in the fray and tried to dig into as many creatures as he could. Bodies of innocent villagers littered the ground, gutted like fish, big holes where their organs had been. Tristan didn't know the creatures enough to understand what they sought, but he could tell they had just encountered some of the Earth's foulest demons.

Then a creature moved from the shadows, its jaws bloody. He backed away, stunned at the sheer amount violence and bloodthirst displayed. Then Blake moved from the side and went right at it – and a fight to the death ensued.

Tristan engaged two other vrykolakas that tried to attack Blake from behind. He thought he'd gotten all of them, panting as he removed the stake from the last one. A gurgle from behind had him freeze. By the time he looked back, Blake was holding his stomach, his eyes wide, face growing paler by the second. He let go... Only to show his intestines. He'd been gutted open, like the rest of the villagers.

"NO!" Tristan roared. He shifted then, taking on the creatures by himself with no care for his own safety. The remainder of the soldiers around them – two or three – did the same and followed his lead. Being in their primal form afforded them a wider range of movements, and protection. There was also the fact his wolf wanted vengeance – and survival.

One by one, the last standing vrykolakas took off – including the one with the white streak. Tristan limped back to Blake's body, dragging his bleeding flank.

His commander looked at him, lifted a hand as if to touch him. "You did good, son," he whispered. Then the hand dropped, and he exhaled his last breath.

Tristan nudged him with his muzzle, but it was too late. The scent of his corpse permeated the air, and the two remaining wolves by his side noticed it as well. Their whimpers echoed his, and they stood in silence for a long moment.

Then Tristan turned his head to the flank and licked it a few times. The healing properties in his saliva did easy work of the wound, and he was able to shift back to human. His gaze fell once more on Blake. He'd been a mentor, a friend, a leader into a world that was darker than most knew. And now...

Tristan didn't get to mourn. Though the creatures had taken off, his remaining companions were there behind him, having also shifted back to human form. "Where do we go from here?"

Blake's unseeing eyes held Tristan's as he felt the weight of the world on his shoulders.

"Home." *Wherever the hell that is.*

∞ ◆ ∞

"Are you sure about this, soldier? Your skills could be of use."

The man behind the desk sounded clichéd, even to a soldier. Tristan arched an eyebrow, trying to avoid being bitter. "Oh, yeah? Even if the shrink called me a nutcase?"

He'd been put through a mandatory psych consult following Blake's death. The human psychiatrist had tried to apply methods and logic to something that defied it, and his advice had been more useless and vapid than this new leader's offer.

When he looked away, Tristan knew what the gesture meant. He gritted his teeth and hissed, "Não, thanks."

He'd given enough.

∞ ◆ ∞

The airport was noisy. Too many people, too many screams. Flashes burst through his head, and Tristan rushed into the nearest washroom. How could it be only minutes since he'd landed, but it felt like he was suffocating? Where else could he go?

Upon exiting, he noticed a sign for trains. His feet moved him there, and before he knew it he'd booked a ticket. At the next station, he took a bus. And before long, he found himself in the middle of nowhere, on a half-empty bus, with only his backpack and wallet.

Sleep took him, but within moments he was awake – biting back a scream. He dug his nails in his palms, forcing his eyes to see past the craziness in his mind, and more into the reality of the night. Nothing helped, and the same creatures he'd hunted flashed in front of his eyes.

By the time he got off the bus, his muscles were protesting, and his eyes felt like he'd rubbed sand over them. The moment he stepped on the ground, though, something shifted. An odd sense of...order.

Without knowing where he was headed, Tristan walked into town - straight for the nearest bar. The neon sign spelled The Cave, and for the first time, a chuckle escaped him. He walked in, ignoring the curious gazes he drew and signaled the bartender. "Scotch on the rocks."

He was served within a moment, and took a seat. Another man was seated near him, and reached out to shake his hand. "Name's Finn McConnell."

Tristan grasped it – and froze. "Tristan Cayne," he managed, trying to ignore what he smelled.

The other grinned. "No need to go all nutter. I caught your scent when you walked in."

Tristan frowned. "What are you?"

"A faoladh." When he shrugged at the name, the Irish said, "A Celtic werewolf. Let's just say I've got a few extra things under my belt."

Tristan smirked at that, thinking of his own abilities. "You may not be alone. I'm a lopisomem."

An eyebrow arched. "No shite... Interesting. So. What brings you here?"

Tristan looked around. "Same as you, suponho. Nowhere else to go."

Finn snorted in his drink and signaled for another. "Got that right, mate."

∞ ♦ ∞

"So what the hell do we do? Stick around?"

Tristan toyed with his drink. They'd been at it for hours, and he felt like he knew the Irish – whatever he was. It still didn't explain why he'd ended up in this town, but then again, life had its ways.

"According to you, we wait. But for what?"

Finn narrowed his eyes at the question, then his expression cleared. "For that."

That same moment, the bar door opened and in walked two other guys. Both were tall, one with dark hair, the other blonde. Identical stubborn expressions. The dark-haired one sniffed the air, then whispered to the other. The blond nodded, then his eyes narrowed in on the bar. They approached slowly.

Tristan stood, muscles corded. The smell rolling off the blond guy... His fingers twitched for a gun, or better yet, a stake. It was a scent he'd caught before. "If it's a fight you want, it's one you'll get."

Finn didn't move from his spot, not really. Yet he reached out to Tristan and tapped his shoulder, as if to get his attention. The touch did something – pulled the tension off him, enough so he grinded his teeth less.

Before he could ask the Irish what he'd done, the dark-haired man smirked. Spreading his palms, he looked at each of them in turn. Then the smirk turned into a cold smile.

"My name is Lucas Bianchi, and I do believe you're on my territory."

Turn to page 123 for a preview

of Tristan's story!

∞ ∞ ∞

EPILOGUE

Nestled between mountains as old as time, under a blood-red sunset, lost amid fog… Was a small house. Shaped on the outside like a regular building with white walls and windows, it had a slightly slanted tip, as if the architect had purposefully decided to throw some chaos into an otherwise symmetrical building. One other thing caught the eye. If one looked at it under the stars, the house sparkled – like a thousand diamonds. And in the sunset light, it appeared bathed in hopes, dreams, and warmth.

Flames could be seen through the windows, and inside it, a couple was slow dancing to a music only they could hear. The man was tall, with wavy blonde hair to his shoulders, eyes the color of the moon, and a face as beautiful as it was impossible to look at. At odds with the environment, he was dressed in a brand-name suit, its darkness in stark contrast to the colorful interior of the house.

The woman in his arms was his complete opposite. Long, wavy brown hair cascaded to her waist, eyes the color of the sun, and a smile as beautiful as spring. As they danced around to the melody of their love, their forms became fluid, like water, and retained a glow about them.

Finally, the dancing stopped, and the man cupped her cheek. "Ileana, draga mea, are you sure about this?"

She leaned into his touch, then rose on her tiptoes and kissed him softly. "I am, Făt Frumos. Dominic is my godson, and if I'm not there to point him in the right direction… Who's to say what will happen?"

The man, Făt Frumos, frowned. "I do not like it."

"Nor I, dragul meu. But if you have survived in the mortal world, and not given in to their temptations, I do believe I can do the same."

Făt Frumos laughed, his head thrown back as a rumble shook his entire body. Then he recovered and leaned his forehead against Ileana's. "You know I only do so, to protect our daughter."

Ileana's smile was brighter than the sun, making her eyes practically glow. "Da, I know. But I miss you."

He moved closer, grasping her waist once more. "And you truly believe love will save them all?"

Ileana glanced around his shoulder to the little fireplace that was burning. In its flames, she could clearly see four men – four wolves – as different as they could be, hanging out in a human bar. Her smile turned speculative. "I believe so, dragul meu."

"Then let that be the last of it," he murmured against her head, and dropped his mouth to hers. "Time for your attention to focus on me alone, iubirea mea."

Ileana's soft laugh echoed the twinkling stars that night…

Preview of First to Fall
(Moonlight Rogues #1)

When the games become real, all bets are off in love and war...

Dominic

I'd been staring at Luz for who knows how long. Hell, years maybe. But something in her called to me as surely as the full moon. Unfortunately, she only has eyes for Lucas. So call me a sucker for punishment, but I'm going to help her. if she wants to draw the alpha's attention, what better way than dating his second in command? Even if it *is* fake.

Lucrezia

Something about Lucas changed, and lately it's all I can do to stop panting after him. Then Dominic comes with this crazy idea: pretend to be his girlfriend, to make Lucas realize he's got the hots for me. And the plan almost works... Until I start falling for the wrong guy. Oh and somewhere in there, find out I live in a town ruled by werewolves. Why can't life ever be simple?

∞ ♦ ∞ **PREVIEW** ∞ ♦ ∞

Lucrezia

My feet crunch in the snow, and for the tenth time this morning I thank my lucky stars I invested in my fuzzy warm boots. It may have been money I didn't have, but with the way the winter is acting up, it will only get worse.

Rockland Creek, Wyoming, is renowned for its harsh winters—not that it's the real reason I ended up here. It was the most remote place near the border with Canada and having that quick escape possible eases the tightness in my back somewhat.

Memories of a much darker time linger at the edge of my consciousness, but I shake them off. Distance and months of breathing freely have made it easier to compartmentalize, and I'm determined to get in to work chipper despite the chilly Monday morning.

An icy gust of wind sweeps up, and I huddle in my coat, wishing I had grabbed an extra sweater underneath it.

Almost there. As if to spite me, Mother Nature throws in some nice flurries—and more wind. Gritting my teeth against it, I quicken my step towards Claws Auto Shop, which I see in the distance. I'm one of those lucky few who can walk to work rather than have to drive or bus, which keeps me in an overall nice shape and clears my mind most mornings.

Most times, it only takes me about half an hour to get there. It's a breeze in summer, but not so much in winter. I vaguely consider asking one of my colleagues for a lift for the rest of the season and then dismiss the idea. The last thing I want them to feel is obligated to protect the only girl in their pack.

By the time I finally reach the side door of Claws Auto Shop, where I work as receptionist, my cheeks are frozen and my fingers refuse to cooperate. I fumble with the key, dropping it three times in the snow, before I get the blasted thing open.

After taking off my coat and switching into some comfortable sneakers, I sit down at my small desk and get started on my day. Within the next hour, as I answer calls and confirm appointments, the guys pile in one by one.

Guys, no. These are *men* and so damn gorgeous my heart hurts every time I notice them. Unfortunately, other body parts I've neglected for a while also poke their head out. Normally, I have a tight control on my hormones. These last few weeks, however...

I tear my eyes away from them and focus on my paperwork, going through the previous week's sales and amounts for collection. Having studied accounting and business while in university, numbers always fascinated me. They make sense, more so than people ever do—to me, at least. But this time around, not even the dry accounts payable booklet is enough to keep me focused. With every ring of the bell announcing someone's presence, I glance up.

First Finn McConnell shows up, his mischievous green eyes twinkling already. With his mop of unruly dark hair and the lithe body of an athlete, he could easily be an actor or model. The lilt in his voice hints at his Irish background, and yeah it's sexy as hell. You would never peg him for a lawyer, but he once dabbled in the trade before leaving Ireland for the States—a long, long time ago like he says.

Next comes Tristan Cayne, brooding about another sleepless night, if the circles under his eyes are any indication. He's a war vet, honorably discharged from the Marines with PTSD—post-traumatic stress disorder. He lost his entire unit in an ambush in the desert and still has the nightmares about it. His skin is tanned even in winter, due to his Brazilian blood, but the man knows how to pull off jeans and a simple shirt like no other. With his shaved head, gentle hazel gaze and square jaw, he's the most aloof of the four.

Third in is Dominic Kosta, with blue eyes that capture me every time and the sinful body of Apollo. Dark blonde hair, clean-cut jaw and muscular build, he's the gentlest of the bunch. At first he told me he was born and bred here, but after many late evening conversations, he revealed he was adopted from a Romanian orphanage by an American couple who couldn't have children of their own.

The story answered a lot of questions about him, and it gave me more insight into this gentle giant who I've seen break more than one heart with all his womanizing. Despite it, there's a quiet confidence in him I respond to, and he puts me at ease in a way no other man has. I've been working here for the last year, but it's Dominic I connected with more than all the others.

His grin lights his face when he sees me, and he moves in for a hug. I squeal out of his grip, shivering at the wind drafting in with him. "Get away, you're ice cold!"

Dom picks me up snorting and twirls me around, before putting me back down. I'm still recovering from the closeness, when the last of them walks in.

"Already wasting time, I see?" Lucas Bianchi's remark would have stung, had it not been delivered with his side-smirk and glittering onyx eyes. The man is Italian to the bone, and his commanding presence tends to leave me shaking at the knees.

Lately, it's morphed into more than that. Whenever he's around, I lose my words—and I haven't crushed on anyone since high school.

"Morning, Lucrezia," he murmurs in his gravelly voice, and I smile feebly in return. To this day, Lucas is the only one who calls me by my full name, all the others having picked up on the nickname Dom gave me: Luz, for light.

As can be guessed, the mixed nationalities have definitely increased my vocab, at least where swearing is concerned. Both Tristan and Lucas lose it in their respective native tongues, and it's almost fun watching them when it happens.

With a nod to Dominic, Lucas heads to the back, already barking orders to Finn and Tristan. Two other guys help around the store in summer, but they're only teenagers from high school, learning the trade. Mostly, it's just us five: me on the paperwork and phones, and the guys tinkering and fixing the cars of Rockland Creek—and of the people passing through.

And I was the lucky one who got to work with them every week, day in and day out.

"Why the long sigh?"

Oops. I'm uncannily aware of Dom's steady gaze on me—and his keen sense of observation.

"Bah, it's Monday," I try to joke, but even I don't fall for it. I peek towards Lucas, who's now opening the doors of the garage—a tell-tale sign announcing they're ready for work.

The inside of their working environment has heat blasting so even with the cool air wafting in, they're comfortable. Not that it seems to matter to these four—they're so hot-blooded a hug from them will have you sweating in no time!

Thankfully for me, a transparent window and well-insulated door separates me from the garage area, and I get to stay indoors and enjoy the warmth.

My gaze is drawn to the two cars already driving in, one of which is a sporty red Mustang convertible. The other is a pickup truck that has seen better days. It's no surprise when Lucas walks over to the Mustang, with Tristan heading to the other car to greet the clients.

"Who the hell drives a car like that in winter?" My eyes narrow in annoyance.

The answer soon makes itself known. A leggy brunette steps out of the car, dressed in dark leggings, thigh-high boots with six-inch stilettos and a white fur coat. Even from afar, I notice her makeup is done to perfection.

Though I'm confident in my flaming locks and exotic features, I don't tend to flaunt my looks. Working with the guys gives me the perfect excuse for casual dress and flying under the radar in jeans and t-shirts.

It's better this way, the reasonable voice in my mind warns. *Remember what happened last time?*

A snort from Dom has me focus back on him, in time to see his grimace.

"What?"

"The girl," he rolls his eyes. "She'll be a handful. I better go, Lucas might need help."

I watch him go, trying to stifle an exasperated sigh—and failing. "You sure it's not *her* you want to get a closer look at?"

Dom turns around at that, a flash of surprise crossing his features. It's gone so quick I might have imagined it. He grins instead and winks. "Not with you around, Luz."

He's gone before I can figure out what he means, and I turn my attention to my regular tasks. At least until the brunette comes for payment. "I was told to come here to pay for the services," she says huskily, and I wonder for a second if she fakes that voice.

I force a polite smile, realizing how mean my thoughts are turning. "Of course. May I see their quote?" She hands me the paper—perfectly manicured nails, I notice—and I plug it into the computer and issue her a formal invoice.

Once she pays I staple a receipt to the invoice and hand it back to her. Eliza Porting is her name, and if it didn't fit her so classically I would laugh about it. She sounds so posh, dresses to a T, yet here she is in the middle of nowhere with a car that broke down.

You once ended up here in a similar way... I try to ignore the reasonable voice nagging me. A lecture would be bad right about now.

Oddly put off, I hand Eliza back the card and return to my computer. I figure this will be it and she'll go wait in the seating area, but she sees fit to hang around.

"How do you work with all that man candy around?" An annoying giggle follows her whispered words.

I track her gaze to the guys, for a moment detracted when Lucas bends down to check under the car, giving us both a perfect view of his, err, assets. Eliza's practically panting in delight, eyes glued to him solely now.

Mine, I want to growl, and hold back. This possessive nature is new for me, as is the jealousy. I have no right, but Lucas is that kind of man. The type you want to lock up and have your way with, day and night... *especially* night.

"Not sure what you mean," I mutter, focusing on papers that need no more organizing.

She turns to peer at me then—really looks at me, assessing me from head to toe—and smirks knowingly. "Oh, I get it. It's okay; I have nothing against people who play for the other team."

The diva goes back to ogling the guys lasciviously, dismissing me in the process. "More for me."

My palm itches, consumed by an almost insane urge to slap her. Just because I dress a certain way, she needs to label me already? *Bitch*.

I'm about to comment, when her next words hit me hard. "So, seen Tommy lately?" Her lips turn upwards into a sneer at my shocked expression, but those eyes are emotionless.

Shit. I thought I escaped this.

Dominic

I stare at Luz for who knows how long this particular time. At first, I tried to keep my distance. She was new, different, and mortal. But something in her calls to me as sure as the full moon, and the more I've known her these last months, the more I want her.

Unfortunately, she only has eyes for Lucas. She doesn't understand the reason for her attraction is linked to his status as chieftain of our pack. Nor that he officially took the lead as alpha in the summer, causing a hell of a lot of hormonal changes in his scent over the last weeks that affect even the most hardened females.

Then again, Luz also has no idea she's living and working in the midst of a town ruled by werewolves.

Some secret, huh?

We've kept it on the down low from the uninitiated—basically, people like Luz who think the world is normal. Her working for us was a complication at first. We were so used to joking around and acting like mutts in heat that needing to censor ourselves seemed like chaining.

It would have built resentment, were it not for Luz's open perspective on life. She quickly—and bossily—got us all in check, ordering us to treat her like one of the guys. It established a certain professional relationship.

Which is why I'm loath to break it. That, and there was something wounded about her when she first appeared in town. I still remember the day she got off the bus with nothing but a backpack, looking lost and so damn vulnerable it tore at my heart. I was in wolf form, and her scent acted like an aphrodisiac I had a hard time letting go of.

Not many humans are supposed to affect us this way. Not many *do*.

Except Luz.

Back then, despite morphing into my human form, I'd still struggled to quiet my wolf down. I can recall, even to this day, the anxiety in her expression when I first asked if she was new to town. After a few moments of awkward talk, I offered to show her around.

It might have been the loneliness or her quick assessment of me, but Luz agreed. Within the day, we ended up at a diner. No matter how much I tried to probe back then—and since then—the only information I got was that she recently moved to Rockland Creek and was searching for a job.

Before I thought things through, I was already telling her our mechanic's shop direly needed a receptionist. Lucas had been none too happy when I showed up with her in tow, but after some discussion, he relented. Luz was hired the next day, and Lucas has admitted on more than one occasion since that it was the best decision he ever made.

My thoughts of Luz must have intruded on my senses because my wolf is growling. *Danger.*

And no, I don't make a habit of hearing voices, at least not in the losing-my-mind way. But I do have a second facet to my personality, and that's my wolf.

He lives within me, like a subconscious part of me, not an alter ego but more… a voice of reasoning. On a regular basis, he pokes his head out only when strong emotions control me, luring me away from my more human side.

But this time…

I listen to the warning and look towards the reception desk where Luz's anger reverberates across the distance. The high-maintenance gal who's with her irks me, and she annoys my wolf.

"Don't," Finn mutters next to me.

I glance at my buddy, surprised he read me so easily. Then again, with Finn, you're an open book more often than not. That's the thing when you're around werewolves with special *gifts*, like I call them.

"You know she has feelings for Lucas." His eyes narrow in disapproval, darting from Luz back to me.

"And you know *why* she has them," I retort, going back to what I'm supposed to be doing—hammering back into shape a beat-up bumper.

Finn follows me to the long table meant for the task, not dropping the conversation. "You're assuming," he accuses, and I hammer the metal a little too hard.

My back muscles tense, and my wolf jumps to defense when I turn to him. "Back off, Finn."

He notices my glare, because after a few tense moments of staring at each other he steps away, hands held up in the air. "I'm only saying, mate. Keep in mind, Luz may have real feelings and more than a crush on our boss."

I don't believe that. *Won't* believe it, is more like it. And as I sense Luz's annoyance go up a notch, my wolf whines. *We can't sit by and do nothing.*

"Need a coffee." My mutter is barely audible, but I don't wait for an answer, instead storming toward the doors. I step through, and the gal from the city moves towards me like a cat pouncing on her favorite toy. Her overwhelming perfume makes me cough and I take a step sideways.

"Aw, poor baby's got a cold?"

I don't know what my face conveys at her idiotic question, but she backs away so fast she almost trips over her heels. "No, just allergic to perfumes, *miss*." I stress the term for professionalism's sake, before dismissing her and turning to Luz.

Luz's eyes flash towards the client and the scent of anger hits me again, something I seldom see in her. It makes the gold stand out against the green of her eyes, and the image of a cat superimposes itself for a moment in my imagination.

Cats and dogs don't mix, my wolf points out. I stifle a smile at that, and Luz stops glaring at the fake Barbie long enough to spare me a concerned look. "You okay, Dom?"

I fake cough this time and force a sheepish grin. "On second thought, I may be coming down with something. Want to make me one of your special teas?"

Whenever any of us is sick, we go to Luz. She has an insane knowledge of herbal teas and their best properties, which comes in handy. My eyes roam over her as she moves from behind the desk, noticing the jeans and long-sleeved purple top she's wearing. She's shorter than me by a head at least, but damn those curves have my mind wandering in a not-so-innocent way, one too many times a day.

Then Luz grins at my words, and it's quick and bright like the sun appearing after a morning of clouds. I swallow past everything else I want to add—this is not the time. Instead, I pout in supplication, hoping the ruse will work.

Luz glances over at the client, undecided and unwilling to slack on the job. "I'll watch her." My promise comes in a mutter, as I'm none too pleased about spending alone time with the snotty client.

After a moment, Luz bites her lip, but relents and moves to the back. "Her name's Eliza."

I'm staring in confusion after her. Why would she give me the useless piece of information? It's not like I'm planning to ask this girl out. Still, once Luz disappears around the corner, I turn to Eliza. "I'm not sure where you think you've landed, miss, but I would loathe rejecting your business because you're upsetting our staff."

She gapes, evidently used to getting her way. *Spoiled*, my wolf snorts, and I can't help but agree when she yells, "Upset your staff? How dare you!?"

The urge to roll my eyes is strong, but I hold back—barely. "In case you haven't noticed, we're a quiet town here. Tight-knit group of people. We notice when someone upsets one of us."

Eliza continues to scowl, but now there's a stubborn lift to her chin as if she's thinking of disputing my words. "Not my fault your girl can't take a joke."

A growl slips past my clenched teeth then, and she widens her eyes.

"Leave. Now."

"You can't do that, I already paid!"

"There is such a thing as a refund," I drawl, crossing my arms over my chest.

"I didn't even *do* anything!" She stomps her foot at that—I wish I was joking, trust me.

"Either you keep your mouth shut around Luz, or I kick you out." When I move towards her, she gives up and sits on the far couch. "Thank you. Now stay there until your car is ready."

I turn away, ignoring her glare, and follow Luz to the kitchen, determined to make sure she's alright.

Lucrezia

Dom's a sweetheart, and his actions warm my heart. Even if he offered to stick around so he could chat up little Miss Princess.

I'm aggravated with myself for caring, and even more so for not being able to let it go. Dom fools around, I know this. He's not a player per se, but he dates enough. In a small town like ours, he's known as a catch—in bed. But never for good.

Enough.

I go about making the honey and cinnamon mixture in the small kitchenette, adding some of the ginger root I keep in the fridge here. Once it steeps enough, I pour it all in a cup and am about to return to the reception area.

I almost smack into Dom, who apparently snuck up behind me and was watching me work.

"Easy," he cups my hands, grabbing the mug from them before it spills and burns me everywhere.

After placing it on the side cabinet, he turns his attention back to me. "You okay?"

I want to answer him, really I do. But I'm struck dumb by his proximity, now in my internal bubble, as I call it. Have I never been this close to him? Or have I only been blind to his charm until today? And why in the hell does it feel like I'm left staring at a real-life Apollo, instead of my best friend?

The broadness of his back seems to dwarf me, and every nerve in my body is aware of our secluded presence. *He could do anything*... My brain tries to backtrack, memories pushing forth, and I half-expect a panic attack.

Yet nothing happens, and that scares me more than the opposite. Either I've lost my mind, or there is something about Dom that makes me feel safe. *Maybe it's because I've known him for so long.*

If I was to reach out, I could touch the muscles of his chest. Even from where I am, heat radiates off him, and something in my stomach unfurls in response.

My breath turns shaky, and this time I can't tell if it's a panic attack, or emotions...or something else.

"Luz, you okay?"

I glance up at his worried tone and manage a nod that's too stiff. "Yeah, fine. Just...out of breath. Sorry."

He frowns then, those beautiful blue eyes warm and scanning me up and down. My skin tingles, and I take a minute to realize he's holding my elbow, as though afraid I'll topple over.

"You sure?"

"Mhm," is my only intelligent answer. Then, like a coward, I side-step him. "Your tea is getting cold," I mutter over my shoulder, and take off the minute he releases his grip.

Dominic

After the morning incident, the day goes by fairly smooth. Eliza leaves with her damn Mustang, and we get no more high class maintenance clients, only our regular clientele. Finn keeps his mouth shut, and I stay busy with as many things as I can take.

Despite my best efforts, I can't stop watching Luz. I see her blush when Lucas asks her out to lunch to go over the sales reports—which they end up doing on the couch in the reception area. I can smell the waves of arousal off her and want to rip his throat out.

Finn steps in at that point, not fooled in the least by my resenting silence. "He's our alpha, Dom."

I ignore how in my face he is, trying to keep my tone curt as I continue to fiddle with the timing belt. "I'm well aware."

"We promised him loyalty."

I throw the piece on the table, ignoring the clank of metal on metal that echoes. I face Finn, failing to appear calm. "He's still new as alpha. And if I recall correctly, I promised him my obedience as his beta, but not my allegiance—and not forever."

Finn glances towards Luz and Lucas, then back at me. "Pack law is clear, mate."

"He hasn't made a claim." The words are more than a growl, but enough to quiet even my wolf.

Then Lucas gets up to go in his office, and Luz watches him with longing. A thought strikes me and before I have time to reason it through, I'm already moving.

This is a terrible idea.

Or so I keep telling myself, even as my feet inch towards Luz. Before I know it, my mouth is running off again—without me. "I can help."

Luz turns those otherworldly eyes to me, the gold more clear up close, and I gulp. I've never had an issue with women, but hell, this one will be the death of me.

"Dom?"

I snap back to with a very unintelligent, "Huh?"

Luz laughs, and I rub the back of my neck.

"Help me with what?" Again, her eyes slide to where Lucas disappeared to.

"With him."

She turns so fast I'm afraid she got whiplash. "What are you talking about?"

"I can help you with Lucas." I drop on the couch, ignoring her stunned expression and those lips I want to kiss so bad my mouth tingles. "You like him, right?"

Her face falls as she whispers, "Am I that obvious?"

"Only to me," I answer truthfully. "But you *do* like him?"

She nods, her eyes big pools of uncertainty.

"Let me help. I know Lucas, we've been buds forever. If he has feelings for you, he may let rules get in the way. Guy always had a thing for not breaking them."

"What rules?"

I want to smack myself—the reference to our werewolf life slipped too quickly. "Dating work colleagues." I save face and change the subject before she inquires further. "Either way, nothing like dating someone to get him to make a move if he's interested."

"I'm not good at dating," she whispers, looking away.

My wolf points its head, sniffing her scent, which changed in a few seconds. *Fear.* I sense it, too. But of what? *Surely it can't be me.* Either way, this is a chance to find out more.

"It won't really be dating. We'll fake it for his benefit. If it makes you more comfortable, we can even put a time limit on it. A week, two weeks, whatever you want."

She glances back again towards Lucas as he steps out of his office and back into the garage. The longing in her expression crushes my heart, but I promise myself to rein it in.

"And what's in it for you?" Her gaze is wary when it meets mine.

I shrug. "A chance to annoy him." *And make you happy. And show you he's not the one for you.* That last part, I don't say out loud.

Luz is silent for so long, I'm sure she'll end up saying no. Besides, what am I thinking? Nothing except selfish thoughts. I want her first kiss, and I want her to at least have the memory of my lips imprinted in her mind before she ends up with Lucas. I want to stake my claim even if it won't be permanent.

"Okay," she surprises me by saying. "How will this work?"

I'm too stunned for a moment to react, but already my wolf is roaring in victory and a grin spreads on my face. "Leave it to me. Meet me tonight for drinks at The Cave, eight o'clock sharp."

When she nods, I lean forward and kiss her cheek, not even surprised when she jumps at the contact. "It'll be fun, you'll see."

And no kidding, I walk away whistling. Yup, like a poor sap who won the girl—not the one who promised to help her get the man of her dreams.

Bite me.

Continue Reading Dom's Story in
First to Fall

Preview of Second to Surrender
(Moonlight Rogues #2)

They say blood is thicker than water...But what if family's the source of your pain?

Tristan

I swore I was done with love, after my last failed relationship. Being a soldier means making the tough decisions, all for the good of the pack. So when a little miss full of attitude waltzes in, dragging a shitload of trouble with her, I want nothing more than to make that tough decision and kick her the hell out. But then she turns those big, helpless eyes on me, and my wolf roars otherwise. Shit-of-fuck but now I'm screwed.... And her family seriously has a screw loose. To make it worse? We have history.

Daniela

You'd think running away from a psycho family would swear me off relationships for good. Guess what? So did I. In fact, I specifically searched Tristan out because he's the type I'd never be with. Too much of everything, if you get my gist – attitude included. So why is it when he starts acting all protector, I can't help but swoon? His dark secrets don't scare me as much as this sudden tornado within me. This was *not* in the plans... And I might just have to make a run for it. But will he let me?

∞ ♦ ∞ **PREVIEW** ∞ ♦ ∞

Tristan

I shouldn't have picked up the damn phone. Better still, I should've thrown it away when I left that cursed town. Why didn't I change my number? Out of some misplaced nostalgia that's now biting me in the ass?

Merda! My hands tighten on the steering wheel and I do everything I can to avoid looking at Dani.

It wasn't meant to be easy, our reunion. Not when she's the exact copy of Izabella. And the last time I'd seen my ex, it had been with her legs up in the air and the pack's beta between them.

"I can feel your anger, you know," Dani whispers.

She's staring out the window, head tilted to the side as if hiding her face from me. And my stomach churns. She doesn't deserve this – paying for her sister's mistake. It was Izabella who drove me out of town, her I have an issue with.

Dani… She's only ever been good to me.

A heavy sigh escapes my lips and I pull the car over to the side of the road. I'm still clenching the steering wheel, taking deep breaths to rein myself in. A tantrum will only spark my wolf into morphing, and that's a pain I don't need right now.

Headlights in the distance come closer, and at first I only notice them out of the corner of my eye. Some stupid car with their lights still on during the day. Then I take a closer look, and the glare sparks another memory.

The headlights. The desert. Middle of the night. So much blood….

"Tristan?"

Dani's voice gets through the fog and I snap to. She's reaching out for me again and I jerk away, slamming into the driver's window. She looks shocked – and I can't really blame her. It's the second time I've done this, without much explanation. But I'm seeing those curls again, the eyes, the mouth, and my mind is somewhere else.

"I'm not her, you know." It's another whisper, this one bitterer.

"I know."

Dani looks away. A beat of silence stretches between us before she finally speaks. "This was a bad idea, but I didn't have a choice. I know you have your new pack, and I was hoping for protection."

The soldier in me stands to attention. "From what?"

A shudder runs through her, and the fear emanating from Dani is tangible, enough to taste. This is the same girl who used to believe in fairies and unicorns when she was young, and promised to forever be by her family's side.

What could have scared her so much, enough to leave Bow's Arrow? The mystery nags at me, and I have a feeling I won't like it when I solve it.

Not that Dani's making it any easier for me. She's silent for so long I don't think she'll answer me. When she does, it's not what I expect.

"You've made it clear I'm an inconvenience, so I won't bother you further. Just bring me to the alpha of this town and I'll plead my case to him directly."

I straighten from my hunched up position by the window. "Dani, I–"

"No." Her eyes flash my way, the amber darker – wary. "I didn't come here to hatch up old history. And judging by your scent, you can't give me what I want anyway. So let's cut the bull, and bring me to your alpha."

Being dismissed like this doesn't come easily, especially not from her. This isn't the young woman I left behind, she's cutthroat and…

"What happened to you?" The question pushes unbidden past my lips, but it's too late to take it back.

Dani's expression shutters and she turns away from me. "I grew up."

Her entire body language is meant to block me. And for a moment, I want nothing more than to shake some sense into her. What no one has done with me, when this gripping dread takes hold of me. But I also know it's the dread that keeps me going, like a comfort blanket.

So I keep further questions to myself and put the car back in gear without a word.

Daniela

I should've known this wouldn't be easy. Heaving back a sigh, I try to tune Tristan out.

It's hard. I haven't been around a werewolf like him for a while, and my senses are tingling. He should be forbidden fruit, but it's not like Izabella's around to care.

And for a moment there, he looked at me – really *looked* at me. Like he saw me, not some ghost of his ex-lover. Maybe things would be settled if he knew the truth once and for all… But I doubt it.

Plus, if Tristan knew everything that happened since he left Bow's Arrow, he wouldn't help me. He'd be too focused on seeking revenge, and probably die in the process. And that's a chance I can't take.

After long moments of silent driving, he pulls in front of what looks like a bar. A neon light spells out The Cave and the building looks old, some colonial antique style. Tristan gets out of the car, and I follow him inside.

"What is this place?" I ask him, expecting he won't answer. "Why are we here, Tristan?"

He throws me a look. "To meet some people." Then he heads in, and I've no choice but to follow.

The place is less crowded than I'd thought. Dismissing the bar, Tristan heads straight for a corner booth where two other guys are seated, along with a female, eating some kind of brunch. Their wolf scents hit me from a distance – except for her. *She's human.*

Tristan stops dead in his tracks and whirls to me. "Yeah, she is. And under the protection of our pack, so lay off it, Dani."

He turns away without giving me a chance to explain and I gape after him. Then I shake myself out of the daze. *This can't be normal, him hearing my thoughts. Can it?*

Something nags at the back of my mind. Our pack was tight-knit, but a connection like this would come only from something deeper. And Tristan left long ago, so there's no way any of that remains between him and any wolf in Bow's Arrow... *If it does, I'm double screwed.*

Instead of focusing on things I can't control, my gaze falls on Tristan's new pack. The redhead is leaning against one of the guys – blonde and blue-eyed, he's a straight Apollo. He notices us first, and surprise flickers in his eyes before a smirk tugs at his lips. Tristan's by their table now, and I reluctantly trail behind him.

"So that's where you disappeared to, mate?" The question's from the second male. With his dark hair and green eyes, I would've pegged him for a Celt even without the Irish lilt in his voice. It makes me uneasy, being around a wolf with his capacities. *If he figures out what I can do...*

"Bite me, Finn," Tristan near-growls. He reaches behind him without looking and grasps my hand, pulling me forward. I nearly stumble into the table, but catch myself in time. It's uncanny how he knew exactly where to reach for me.

Oblivious to my stupefaction, Tristan introduces me. "This is Daniela Da Silva, an old friend. She needs to speak to Lucas. Where is he?"

Three pairs of interested eyes turn on me, but it's the redhead who speaks first. She stands and smiles broadly, holding out her hand. I hesitantly shake it. "I'm Lucrezia – but everyone calls me Luz. This is Dominic – Dom – Konstantin, my boyfriend, and Finn McConnell." She introduces first the blonde-haired guy by her side, then the Celt.

I nod at each of them, then bite my lip. How much does she know, and what can I say in front of her? This is why I avoid packs. Especially packs with mated females. The bond between her and Dom is strong enough even I, a stranger, can feel it.

The Celt speaks next, probably sensing my discomfort. "Luz knows about us, so feel free to speak your mind around her."

A relieved sigh escapes me. "I've travelled a way from my old town, and I'm afraid only your alpha can help. Is he around?"

I notice the glance between Dom and Tristan, before his light blue eyes settle on me. "Lucas is unavailable for the day, perhaps a bit longer. Other business has him occupied. I'm his beta, perhaps I can help?"

While I appreciate the thought, I'm shaking my head before he's done. "I'm here to ask for protection, but the details are too sensitive to share around." I bite my lip again. "The less you know, the better off you'll be."

Rather than dissuade them, my words only spark curiosity in all of them. *Shit.*

Tristan snorts by my side and mutters something akin to, "Welcome to my world." Then he addresses Dom. "I'll get Dani a drink."

"She could join us," Luz offers.

They may not see the tension in Tristan, but I do. And the last bit of hope I had about him being okay with my presence here crumbles to dust. "It's okay," I smile feebly, then turn to the bar before they can see my tears.

"Two whiskeys," Tristan orders by my side, then takes a seat next to me. I guess people in Rockland Creek make it a habit of drinking during the day, because the bartender doesn't even blink.

"I don't need you to babysit me," I whisper into my drink.

"Doubt that."

His mutter aggravates me more than I can say. I throw back the drink, then stand. Even with me upright, we're barely eye level. Damn him and his height – and those *malditos* broad shoulders that draw my attention every two seconds like clockwork.

"You know what, Tristan? Call me when your alpha's around. I don't want to *impose* in the meantime."

His eyes narrow on me, glinting molten chocolate in this light. "What the hell are you going on about, carinho?"

I shove his chest – hard. Not that it has any effect on him. "Don't freaking call me darling. I'm not Izabella."

He stands at that, his eyes flashing. "You think I don't know that? I'm not delusional, Daniela."

"Really? 'Cause from where I'm standing, you're definitely not in your right mind." I take a step back, scanning him up and down. "Matter of fact, you sure you're fit to be rescuing anyone?"

Tristan growls, and I distinctly hear his teeth snap together. "You have no idea what you're talking about."

"Really?"

He shakes his head, then downs the rest of his drink. "I came when you called, didn't I? Should earn me a measure of trust, if nothing else."

I shake my head. "It was a mistake. You shouldn't have. You and I – we have nothing." Having delivered my scathing reply and gotten the satisfaction of seeing the startled look in his eyes, I walk away.

Tristan

I'm still standing like a dumb idiot when someone taps my shoulder, drawing my gaze away. Luz's red curls and green eyes greet me. There's a twinkling in their depths that spells trouble for me.

"So, friend, huh?"

My jaw clenches at her words and I look back to the other side of the bar, where Dani's resolutely ignoring me. *How in hell...* I can't. I look at her, but it's another I see. And I. Can't. Disassociate.

Fuck me.

Another poke, this time more insistent, focuses me back on the fiery redhead by my side. I glance around the bar, looking for Dom. He needs to come and gather his mate, but he's too busy looking smug and leaning against a wall.

He doesn't have to speak for me to get his meaning. *You're on your own.*

Screw you too, buddy.

Dom shrugs, and Luz pokes me again.

"What?" I unclench my teeth long enough to spit it out.

She grins as if I've just awarded her the best gift. "Nothing..." Her eyes flicker to Dani, and the grin widens. "She's pretty."

So is her twin, who broke my heart.

The words are on the tip of my tongue, but I bite them back and grunt instead. Luz rolls her eyes, more than used to our caveman ways by now – or so I'd hope, considering the wolf she's shacking up with.

As if on cue, Dom finally moves off the wall and joins us. His arm wraps around Luz, pulling her back against his chest. She melts into him, and I look away. Needing to escape their love, their connection that stirs my wolf. He demands one of his own – and my eyes land on Dani, again.

Merda.

"She's got you twisted already? Now that's a record if I ever saw one."

I scowl back at Dom. "You've no idea what you're talking about, meu amigo."

"Hmm." Dom arches an eyebrow. "I may not be Finn, but that's a helluva spitfire you have there. Plus, she's from your old pack, meaning she gets your crazy shit. You can't ignore a girl like that." His gaze falls on Luz. "Trust me, I know."

A snort escapes me, and my expression eases. "I've no intention of chasing her."

"And why not?" Something about Luz's question gives me pause. Her eyes are inquisitive, as if she understands there's something holding me back.

Not that I can talk about it. "We've got history, her and I. And not in the way you're thinking, Lucrezia. It's…complicated."

Her green eyes are a little too eager, and I refuse to explain myself. *Screw it.* I signal the bartender for another shot, and practically rip it from his hand. I'm not like Dom and the others – alcohol *does* get to me. It doesn't make me drunk, but it numbs everything – my senses, my nightmares, my wolf.

And right now, I need it. So I gesture for another. Luz whispers something to Dom, who rests his hand on my shoulder. I shrug it off.

There's a guy getting closer to Dani, talking to her and offering to buy a drink from the way he's gesturing. A growl escapes me, and Luz's chuckle half-registers.

"He's a goner."

"Would you two get a life?" It's thrown over a shoulder, because I'm already moving towards trouble.

Daniela

I feel him standing behind me, but don't turn around. Instead, I increase the charm up a notch and focus all my attention on the guy. He was nice enough to buy me a tequila shot – which I downed like there's no tomorrow. A second followed. And a third.

Numbness is the name of the game right now. It's all I'll have tonight, and I need it more than anything. Probably not the best way to deal with problems, but try being me for a second. With a family as fucked up as mine is, I'm better off forgetting.

Plus, why should I give Tristan the time of day? I mean, I hadn't expected him to actually be nice to me, considering what Izabella put him through, but some acknowledgement of a friendship we'd shared a while back would have been better than this.

The hurt makes my insides clench, but I keep on a neutral expression for my companion. He's a nameless face right now, designed to keep my mind off the one wolf it shouldn't linger on.

My mark throbs again, and I move my hand to rub it. Time is running out, or it did as soon as I left Bow's Arrow. And they'll come looking for me. My eyes close against the wave of despair threatening to overwhelm me.

There's a thought, a darker one, that goes on a loop in my head. *What the hell am I going to do if Tristan doesn't listen, if I can't get protection here?*

As if sensing my doubt, another wave rises within me. Only, it's not despair. It's something very, very tangible. It rumbles within me, eager to come out. Panic freezes me, before I jump into action, motioning for the bartender to serve me another drink.

It's a temporary solution, but I don't intend to show my hand in this bar full of wolves. It'd be suicide, for one. For another, I definitely wouldn't be getting any protection out of it.

So yeah, the tequila helps by keeping everything at bay. At least, until Tristan speaks.

"Can I talk to you?"

I don't bother turning around. "Nope, I think we're done for the night. Call me if your alpha resurfaces."

Silence only answers, then the growl at my back pulls me out of any wayward thoughts. Before I can tell him to piss off, Tristan grabs my arm and jerks me off the barstool. Then he drags me behind him and through the doors heading at the back.

In the distance, I see Luz leaning against Dom. They're both watching us and smiling like they know a secret I don't. And hell if I don't wonder what it is.

Then we're outside, and it's pouring rain. Cold rain, in the middle of winter. It's darker outside, way too dark for only mid-afternoon now. I glance upwards at the sky, noticing the thundering clouds. A shiver runs through me, but it has nothing to do with the weather. My werewolf blood keeps me warm enough.

No, what really scares me, is what I see perched atop a building – a raven. Its moonshine eyes are fixed on us, head tilted to the side like it's listening. Panic seizes me again, and I try to run back inside. But Tristan is faster.

"Stay," he growls. "We need to talk, away from prying eyes."

My gaze lifts again to the raven. Its beady eyes are still on us. I shake my head, trying to rip myself from his grip. "Let me go, Tristan!"

He frowns, his eyes scanning me up and down. We're both soaked through our jeans and jackets now, and my hair is plastered to my face. But still he looks, until I'm forced to meet his gaze. And the burning fire in it scorches me.

"Tristan, I—"

Something snaps in him, and I swear I hear it. Before I can draw another breath, he pushes me against the wall. I yelp when my back hits it, but his mouth falls on mine. And trust me when I say, I don't pull back from it.

Continue Reading Tristan's Story in
Second to Surrender

Preview of Third to Tumble (Moonlight Rogues #3)

Rules are meant to be broken... Unless breaking them tears an entire family apart.

Finn

I'm the cool headed one. The rule-follower. The non-hormonal-raging wolf.

This pack needs someone like me. We've fought creatures of the night, stuck together through psychotic families and dealing with magic and the unbelievable. We're all thick as thieves, and the worst thing that could happen is getting kicked out of this pack.

Breaking rules is not my thing.

So why does Elle make me want to throw it all away?

And why is it my stupid, idiotic wolf does exactly that...before I've even had a taste of her lips?

Elisandra

He barges in like he owns my destiny, and yeah it's hot as sin. That Irish accent, those gorgeous eyes, it'd be easy to fall for it.

Only I don't. I may look as sweet as the baked goods I sell, but there are thorns under this armor Finn has no idea about.

And then things get really complicated when Tytus is added to the mix, telling me stories I can't believe. They're fables, myths....aren't they? 'Cause if they're not, those thorns I mentioned may just burn down this entire town.

∞ ♦ ∞ **PREVIEW** ∞ ♦ ∞

Elisandra

The damn delivery truck had to crap out on us – again. Grandmama's already had a hard enough time with grandpa gone and now... *Ugh.*

And of course there's only one damn mechanic shop in this town, and *he* happens to work there. I wish it didn't make a difference. That he didn't make my pulse race, my heart beat faster, nor create butterflies in my stomach. I wish I didn't think of him naked whenever I see him. I wish to hell I was indifferent.

Only, I'm not.

Finn McConnell. Tall, lean, eyes the color of the lush emerald landscape he's from, a jaw I could trace time and time again. And that Irish lilt that melted me to pudding the first time I heard it.

I never had a chance.

Oh, I've seen him around. Since he showed up to town, I've seen him. And the guys he hangs out with, each hotter than the last. Only, Finn doesn't even know I exist.

Which is why it's even harder dragging the damn car there and making my way inside the shop. A reception desk is set up outside the garage doors. A familiar redhead's typing furiously, while the new girl in town chats animatedly. They're dating two of Finn's best friends – Dom, and Tristan. And no, I'm not a stalker. I just…see.

They both look up when I enter, and I hesitate, shifting from foot to foot. "Do you guys have room for one more appointment today?" I don't tell them it's urgent. That grandmama depends on this. I can't appear *that* desperate.

As they share a look, a loud clatter startles me – it's coming from the garage. And then I feel *his* eyes on me.

Don't look. Don't look. Don't —

I look. It's impossible not to, like a damn magnet. My gaze travels through the transparent door into the garage and collides with Finn's emerald gaze. A faint flush creeps up his neck, then he picks up the tool he dropped and bends back over the car. Now my eyes are glued to his corded back, showcased in a dirty white shirt over equally dirty jeans. As he messes with something in the engine, his muscles tense and release. *He's screwing something there.*

Wish he'd screw us.

I jump at the voice. *This* is why I can't be around Finn. She always shows up, without a fault, and I'm having a harder time keeping a rein on her.

It's not that I'm possessed. But, there's something wrong with me, alright. 'Cause that voice in my head, it's me – only a nastier version.

Just one bite. Look at that ass.

And did I mention sluttier version?

No, I scowl, noticing my reflection on glass pane darkening. It's not the first time I've had full conversations in my head, but I try to force myself to look at Lucrezia and Daniela instead. They've been awfully quiet, observing me with mirroring interested expression.

"Sorry, I'm a bit scattered today. Um, so, do you?"

Lucrezia nods and grins. "Absolutely! What's the issue?"

"Transmission crapped out on me." I hate asking, but it's a must-know at this point. Grandmama's business isn't in top shape, and since she went up to visit her sister and stayed there, it's gotten worse. Only, I can't tell her how bad, since she'll want to come back. So I bite on my pride and say, "Any idea how much it'll cost?"

Lucrezia types something in, then shakes her head. "No, but once Finn has a look he can give you an estimate."

I dig my nails into my palms, refusing to surrender to the temptation of looking his way. "Is there anyone else who could check it out?"

She glances up with a small frown. "I...maybe?"

Daniela, quiet up until then, says, "We can probably rope of the other guys in, but it may take longer."

Just my luck.

Yummy luck!

Shut up.

Sighing, I nod. "Never mind, then. Anyone will do, but I need this fixed ASAP. We have a baked goods delivery for a wedding out of town and....it's important nothing delays it, Lucrezia."

A small frown creases her features. "Of course. And I told you to call me Luz, no need for the mouthful my name is." When I only answer with a weak smile, she gets up. "We'll do our best, I promise. I'll go get Finn so he can take a peek right away."

"No, stay," Dani smirks. "I'll go." When she passes me, she stops and says, "I'm Dani, by the way. I don't think we've ever been formally introduced."

I shake her hand, envying her confidence as she struts up to Finn.

Finn

This makes three.

Three times I've made a complete fool of myself around this girl – Elle.

Elisandra Worthington. I know because I've made it my business to know. Not that it helps. This is one bird I can't figure out for the life of me. She's shy as all sights, but handles an entire bakery by herself – her grandma hasn't been around in a while. And while I can't explain my interest in her, I'm also oblivious to why my wolf has suddenly decided it wants to stake his claim on her.

I want to blame Dom and Tristan. These blokes were first to fall and now here I am, feckin' tumbling head first into something I'm nowhere ready for.

Jerking at the machinery that just won't give today, I try to angle my thoughts elsewhere. It's impossible, at least while she's in the same building. There's something about Elle, yeah. And the way her burning stare is glued to my ass right now, focus flies out the window – as does the screwdriver in my hand. Again.

"Look who's all clumsy today."

The breathy voice takes me by surprise. I'm not usually this unaware, especially with females around me. It's with a sigh that I turn to Dani.

"No more than usual."

She cocks a hip against the car I'm fixing and smirks. "Yeah? So, it's got nothing to do with the pretty brunette who just walked in?"

My treacherous eyes shift again to Elle. She's squirming, uncomfortable in whatever conversation she's having with Luz. "What did you two say to her?"

The words come out more cross than I'd intended. Dani's smirk widens. "Não, meu amigo.

We said nothing. Seems sweet Elle is just as much of a mess around you."

Damn.

My gaze moves to Elle again. Our eyes lock across the distance and a zing goes through me, like I've been electrocuted.

Yummy.

The word rings in my head as clear as if she'd spoken. Elle's eyes widen, then she breaks the stare and tries to rush out the door.

"Finn, wait!" Dani's voice echoes behind me, but I'm already gone.

Don't let her leave, or you may not see her again. The impulse is strong – too impossible to resist. So I burst through the side garage door and intercept Elle as she tries to flee.

"Running off, love?" I hope to high hell and beyond she doesn't see through the front I'm putting up.

Elle looks at me then, her lips parted. The moment lengthens, and I taste her interest, mixed with something else. It's everywhere in the air. And it's such a sweet invitation, I'm about to take it despite myself – until her eyes flash.

And it's enough to make me pause. Because I've seen that look before...in one I hate.

Then I realize she's talking to me. "Sorry, what?"

She crosses her arms over her chest then, scowling at me. "I said I wasn't *running*, you just seemed busy." A pause, then, "Lucrezia said you might have room for one more appointment."

I follow her gaze to the minivan parked near the auto shop. "What's wrong with it?"

"Transmission, I think."

Elle's voice is soft now, less edgy than before. Her emotions are too chaotic to place, but one thing I'm sure of. This attraction isn't one-sided.

Which is why my feckin' mouth runs off without me and says, "I'll have a look."

Elisandra

Yum.

Ugh she won't shut up. And I'm probably not helping by checking Finn out every two minutes. What the hell possessed me to stick around?

Grandmama's business, that's what. She and grandpapa took care of me after my parents died. And now, well, somehow it seems only fair I help out.

Double yum.

"Ugh, would you shut up?"

Lucrezia stops typing and looks up. "Sorry?"

"No, not you." I cringe. "Can't really say I've got a voice in my head that only comes out when Finn's around, can I?"

Her eyes go wide. My stomach sinks.

"I didn't just..."

"Say that out loud?" She grins. "You so did."

"Crap." I bury my head in my hands, taking a deep breath through my fingers. *Could this day get any worse?*

Lucrezia comes and sits next to me, rubbing my shoulder. "No shame in it. He's something, alright."

I peek out from my hands. "Please don't say anything."

"Of course not!."

"I'm not usually this crazy."

Lucrezia smiles. Then her eyes go over my shoulder and the smile turns into something blinding. I envy that joy, and the soft welcome in her voice when she says, "Hey."

"Draga mea."

The deep voice – I know it. It's Dominic, her boyfriend. Lucrezia stands and goes to him, burying herself in his embrace. It's not long before Tristan and Daniela walk in, interrupting the moment with their loud bickering.

"I said não, beleza, why don't you listen?"

"Because Lucas is already impossible and you know I can help! If I've got this ma—"

Lucrezia clears her throat noisily and Daniela stops mid-sentence. Her eyes fall on me. "Elle! Still around?"

It's not said in a mean way, but I still get defensive. "Just waiting on a quote, Daniela."

"Call me Dani." She cranes her neck around Tristan and grins at Finn. "Taking his sweet time, I see."

It's then I'm aware of both Dominic and Tristan's heavy gazes on me. They share a look, and Dominic gives a small shrug, as if answering a silent question. Then he kisses Lucrezia. "I'll be back. Need to run an errand with Tristan."

"Again? But you just got back!"

He shrugs in apology and they take off, but not before Tristan lingers around Dani, kissing her a few times. I look away, scorched by their intensity. Then the guys are gone once more and Luz and Dani's chatter dies away.

I'm once more drawn to Finn. His form, his right *everything* moving around...

"Did you know he used to be a lawyer?"

I snap out of my daze at Luz's words.

"Who, Finn?" The way Dani asks it makes it seem like she's overdoing it for my sake.

"Yeah, back when he lived in Belfast."

"Why'd he move here?"

Luz shrugs at my question. "Never did find out. He keeps to himself."

Dani snorts. "Speak for your experience."

A glance passes between them. Then I turn to look at Finn again. Another voice draws my attention. "Che cazzo... What the hell is *she* doing here?"

Finn

Crap. This'll cost a pretty penny. And something tells me from the state of this car, it won't be easy for Elle to come up with the funds. Then again, that's not my problem. I shouldn't care. Nor should I care that I've felt her eyes on me the last hour.

Ruckus by the reception area draws my wolf. He's always a bit too damn interested when people exhibit too many emotions.

My mouth parts as I taste their scents. See, most wolves focus on their nose, but my ancestry gave me something different. I can taste everything – desire, anger, embarrassment.

Like Dani, who's annoyed she's being left behind. Dom and Tristan have been out patrolling the last few days since the fight with the Reapers and her old pack. We don't want to be taken unawares, not that it's helped much. And Dani, naïve in some ways, doesn't understand Lucas is purposefully keeping her in the shop to protect what's here – Lucrezia.

As an indoctrinated member of our pack, she's the only human around us. And since the Reapers hate humans, Lucas thinks they might come after her – our weakest link.

Of course, his Italian macho side also wants to keep the women away from whatever horrifying discoveries Dom and Tristan run into on their patrol. With the Reapers crazy and Cade as their leader, the town itself is changing.

All thoughts of change leave my mind when Lucas steps into the reception area. I'd feel his anger even without my extrasensory perceptions. *Shit.*

Dropping the clipboard I was writing my estimate on, I make my way to them.

"....and Finn's just getting an estimate. Won't be long now."

I walk in at the last of Luz's babbling. "Problem, boss?"

For Elle's sake, we have to try to keep it normal. I can taste her wariness and sense of doing wrong.

Get her out of here.

The voice is loud in my head – demanding. It's an order if I ever heard one. I focus on Lucas' glare. "It'll be a complicated job, but I've got room."

Lucas looks to Elle, dismissing me. "Afraid we're capped out for the week." He doesn't sound the least bit apologetic.

Elle's face falls. "Are you sure? What if I pay double?"

Something tells me it's a bluff. Not that it changes Lucas' mind. "Scusi, but it's a hard *no*." Then the heartless bastard walks off.

Elle looks ready to burst into tears, and my reaction gets the best of me again. I step closer to her, touching her shoulder. She jumps as if jolted, and I pull my hand back, frowning at it. *Yeah, I definitely sensed that zap again.* Despite my confusion, I whisper, "It'll be okay. We'll do it, just give me a second to sort the schedule out with my boss."

Ignoring the gratefulness in her eyes, I stalk after Lucas. "Why are you being so nutty all of a sudden?"

Lucas throws me a glare over his shoulder. "Not you, too. I need one wolf at least with a clear head!"

My steps slow down. "Have I ever disappointed?"

Lucas stops moving away, and sighs rather dramatically. Pinching the bridge of his nose, he turns to me and stares, not saying anything.

He doesn't have to. When Dom fell in love, he broke all the rules – and then some. All to claim Lucrezia. When it was Tristan's turn, he fell so hard and so fast for Dani, he didn't even see it coming. Nor did he know what to do with it – other than challenge his alpha at the most idiotic of times. And as for me...

I'm not there yet. Nor do I plan to be.

So I say the words I know will get Lucas to budge. "She's just a girl. An inconsequential nobody, boss. Let me do the job and she'll be out of our hair."

His onyx eyes glitter. "It's not a simple job, is it?"

"No. But I'll pay it out of pocket if I have to."

"That won't be necessary."

Shit.

I turn and sure enough, there's Elle behind me. *How much did she hear?*

The hurt on her expression tells me she caught more than enough.

<u>Continue Reading Finn's Story in</u>
Third to Tumble

Preview of Last to Love
(Moonlight Rogues #4)

**He's the last one standing... Which is why they
sent the best one to break him.**

Lucas

Love is for fools. I left all that crap behind,
and no fairy-like, smiling godmother will change my
mind. My wolves are falling in love like bowling
pins, and no amount of reasoning will make them
stop.

Now the last one's gone over the moon, and
they all expect me to be the last to love.

Only they've got another coming.

'Cause the only way I'm falling in love?

Over my own dead body.

Monica

One more job, they said. One tiny thing I have
to do, to bring the prodigal son back home in the
warms of his beloved family. They said it would be
easy. They gave me all the tools.

But the minute I'm facing Lucas, I know all
those plans have just failed. Burned, thrown out the
window, type of failed.

Those onyx eyes see right through me, and I
fully expect he'll throw me out on my ass. So why is
it he's suddenly more interested in getting me in bed

than thrown out? And what happens when I fall for it...

∞ ♦ ∞ **PREVIEW** ∞ ♦ ∞

Lucas

Matteo. Francesca. A past as buried as it is painful...

All that flashes in my mind when Monica bursts into my office. I'm not fool, and her scent is too easy to determine. And yet, despite my inner turmoil, I manage to keep my regular neutral expression.

"Leave us."

Finn glances at me, and I don't know how much my faoladh friend has sensed of my reaction. I can only hope he keeps whatever he did feel to himself.

My gaze narrows on the brunette the minute he's gone through the door.

"And who are you?"

"Monica Delucci," she says, swinging her hips as she walks to my desk, then takes a seat uninvited. "Your parents sent me."

Coldness sweeps through me at her admission, but I mask my emotions before they get the best of me. "Did they, now?"

Monica

Damn it, but they could have warned me what to expect!

Luciano Conti is nothing I expected. He's gorgeous, and fine as hell, sure. But he's also cold, and unsettling. And in control. I didn't miss the way his wolf responded, nor the pack outside of here. Clearly, I've walked in the middle of a warzone.

The question is, how much more chaos can I cause before Luciano – or Lucas, as he calls himself now – throws me out of here? I bite my lower lip, noticing his gaze drop to it. My instructions were clear. Ruin the life he built here, and force him to come back home. If I did, I'd be queen to his king, and Alessandro Conti would ensure it.

Only problem is, as I'm standing opposite Luciano, it takes all my will to ignore the hum of electricity between us.

In an effort to distract myself, I look around. "You've done well for yourself, Luciano. Your parents will be proud."

A noise escapes him, and I meet his unnerving gaze just in time to catch a glimpse of amusement. Then he schools his expression once more.

"What was so funny?" He clearly doesn't like my question. But it's his words that unsettle me more.

"Funny you keep mentioning parents, as if I have two of them. My mother died years ago. Matter of fact, she committed suicide after my brother died in a failed deal – all thanks to my father. But surely Alessandro Conti told you all this, before sending you in the wolf's den?"

His grin is nothing short of predatory. And that dangerous glint in his onyx eyes causes a low tremor to start in me.

Shit. I've been had, that's for sure. Only question is, how the heck do I get out of this now?

Continue Reading Lucas's Story in

Last to Love

About the Author

Alexa Whitewolf was born in Romania a little after the fall of Communism, 1992 to be exact. Growing up in the Transylvania region surrounded by epic mountains and a never ending stream of legends and stories was bound to create an overactive imagination. From a young age, she started rescuing pets–abandoned dogs in warehouses, kittens about to be drowned–and spent her childhood talking to animals. This devotion to the furry creatures shows up in her writing, as most of her series will have one– or more–pets involved (think Alistair if you read The Avalon Chronicles, Tyr in The Sage's Legacy).

The move to Canada in her teens was a sometimes rough adjustment, and Alexa overcame it by burying herself in books–both reading and writing. She started her young adult series at that time, and continued with the fantasy of Avalon in university. Nowadays? She's working on a few other upcoming series, among which a werewolf paranormal romance.

Alexa currently lives nearby picturesque Ontario, where Starbucks locations abound. When not at home writing–or awake in the middle of the night trying to put her characters to sleep–Alexa can be found enjoying walks with her husband and two masters of mischief, Zeus and Achilles. Her social media feed is always inundated with animal posts, so if you're looking for some sunshine in your day, you know where to find it: Facebook, Twitter or Goodreads, so don't be shy!

When the mood strikes, Alexa also dabbles in handmade jewelry and stationery for special occasions, as well as the occasional website creation for friends. And if that's not enough to keep this night owl busy, she's still trying to convince her husband to get another puppy–sadly, a work in progress.

You can read more on her books, enter giveaways and follow her blog on travel, dogs and life in general at **www.alexawhitewolf.com**

Be sure to sign up for Alexa's mailing list for exclusive perks!

Also by the Author

The Avalon Chronicles series
Avalon Dreams
Avalon Wishes
Avalon Nightmares
Atrox – A novella

The Sage's Legacy – YA series
The Dragon Medallion
The Dragon Manuscript
Relics of the Underworld

Moonlight Rogues series
First to Fall
Second to Surrender
Third to Tumble
Last to Love

Standalone novels
Blood Ties, Love Binds
Unconditional Love
Blazing in a Storm of Ashes (Coming soon)

Sign up for my readers' group at
www.alexawhitewolf.com/contact and receive a
copy of *Unconditional Love* for FREE, as well as
first dibs on cover reveals, discounts, giveaways,
prizes and more!